FAR NORTH

WILL HOBBS

AN AVON CAMELOT BOOK

AVON BOOKS, INC.
1350 Avenue of the Americas
New York, New York 10019

Copyright © 1996 by Will Hobbs
Published by arrangement with William Morrow and Company, Inc.
Library of Congress Catalog Card Number: 95-42686
ISBN: 0-380-72536-3
www.avonbooks.com

First Avon Camelot Printing: September 1997

CAMELOT TRADEMARK REG. U.S. PAT. OFF. AND IN OTHER COUNTRIES, MARCA REGISTRADA,
HECHO EN U.S.A.

Printed in the U.S.A.

OPM   20   19   18   17   16   15   14

to the Dene of today and tomorrow

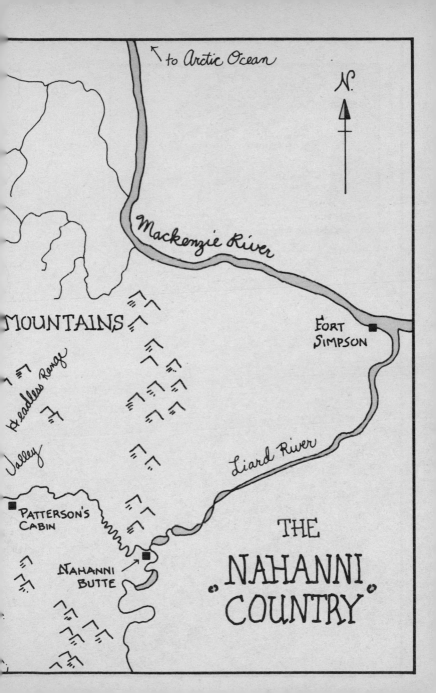

The first I ever heard of the Nahanni River and Deadmen Valley was from the bush pilot who met my flight at Fort Nelson, way up at the top of British Columbia. Clint worked for an air charter service that was trading out a favor for my father by flying me on to Yellowknife, the capital of Canada's Northwest Territories.

"Gabe Rogers?" he asked doubtfully as I stepped off the plane.

"Clint?" I asked just as doubtfully. "You're the bush pilot?"

This guy was about twenty-two, that's the oldest I'd give him. Big grin, friendly as a puppy dog, big head of curly blond hair, and a square jaw with a dimple in it. He said, "You talk just like your dad—Texas accent and all. I was expecting you to be tall like your dad, too, eh?"

"Nobody's as tall as my dad," I said. "That's why they call him Tree."

A mischievous grin spread across the young bush pilot's face. "Anybody ever call you Stump?"

I had to laugh. "Not until now, but there's a first time for everything."

"I've seen some big guys on those drilling rigs, but nothing like your dad, eh? Your shoulders sure remind me of his—wide as an ax handle. You wrestle?"

"Wrestle and play football. I was a running back."

"Hockey's my game—you ought to try it. Hey, guess what. Another pilot took off with my airplane—there's a forest fire going on north of here, up in the Yukon."

"So how do we get to Yellowknife?"

"Well, the company's got a van stuck here at Fort Nelson, and now they figure I'm just the guy to drive it back to Yellowknife."

"How far's that?"

"Oh, only about six hundred miles."

We piled my gear into the van, an old Suburban armored with red dirt and a windshield that looked like it had been through a war. On a wide gravel road that stretched endlessly ahead through a forest of shaggy spruce trees, Clint buried the gas pedal, leaving behind a contrail of dust. It looked as if he intended to drive to Yellowknife in the same time it would have taken to fly there. I glanced nervously at the speedometer. He was already doing 115 kilometers per hour, whatever that was. It sure felt fast on the gravel, and I started to wonder if this guy was going to kill me, but I didn't say anything. I tried to relax, figuring that was just the way people drove in Canada.

"This road didn't even exist ten years ago," Clint said with pride. "The first thing you should know about the Northwest Territories is that it's *big*. It stretches from the Yukon practically to within spitting distance of Greenland. The N.W.T. is twice as big as Alaska."

In that case, I thought, Texans have absolutely no bragging rights in the North. "That's big," I agreed, as my eye went back to the speedometer. He was up to 125 kilometers per hour.

"See if you can picture this: only sixty thousand people live in the entire N.W.T., and almost a third of them live in the city of Yellowknife."

I was taking in the scale of one tiny corner of it in the green blur rushing by the passenger window, the big emptiness and the strangeness. For a kid from the Texas hill country, this world of the northern forest seemed like something you'd read about in a book and wonder if it could possibly be real. I felt good about my decision to come try it. It might be rugged up here, but I could already tell it wasn't going to be boring.

Clint was steering left-handed down a long straight-away with only a couple of fingers on the wheel, while his right hand was fiddling with a yellow fishing jig in a tackle box between us. A hundred and forty kilometers per hour, that's what the speedometer was reading now. The van didn't feel very attached to the gravel. It felt more like we were floating. Back in Texas, my grandparents drove so slow it made me crazy. That wasn't a problem with Clint. "So how does kilometers per hour compare to miles per hour?" I asked him as casually as possible.

"Ten kilometers is right around six miles."

I did the math in my head. The answer scared me, so I did it over. I was right the first time: eighty-four miles an hour. To get my mind off Clint's driving, I asked, "What's the deal with the trees turning gold and red already? It's still August."

"Those are aspens and paper birch. Another eight or nine weeks, and the hammer comes down."

"The hammer?"

3

"Winter! Welcome to the Northwest Territories!"

"What's that mean, 'hammer'?"

"Sledgehammer!" He laughed. "The cold and the darkness, that's the hammer, and the land, that's the anvil. There's practically three hours less daylight now than there was a month ago."

"Too bad I missed summer."

"So you're starting school in Yellowknife?"

"Tenth grade."

"From what I hear, those residential schools are no picnic."

"I'll make out all right. I wanted to be closer to my father."

"While he's working the diamond boom and making the big bucks, eh? Your mother's back in Texas?"

"I've been living with my grandparents in San Antonio while my dad's been up here. My mother's dead."

"I didn't know. I'm sorry."

"I was only seven. Car wreck—drunk driver."

For a couple of minutes Clint didn't speak. Maybe he slowed down a little. Then he pointed off to our left. "That's the southern edge of the Mackenzie Mountains. Ever hear of 'em?"

"All I know about Canada I learned in the old Bullwinkle cartoons."

"That's the way of it, eh? We Canucks know you, but you Americans, all you think of when you think of Canada is moose, right?"

"I guess so," I agreed.

"Well then," Clint said thoughtfully, "just for the sake of argument, let's say all of Canada is one big old moose. Then, what you Americans really know about

4

us, that would compare to about the size of . . . a moose dropping.''

"Interesting way to put it," I said. I was trying to visualize a moose dropping, having never seen one before.

"Anyway, I was going to tell you about the Mackenzie Mountains. In July I flew a couple of canoe parties back in there. They were going to paddle out of the mountains on the South Nahanni River.''

"Did they make it?" I joked.

"Hey, no guarantees. . . . It's sometimes called the River of Mystery for all the strange things that have happened back there. And everything's huge. The Nahanni's got a waterfall on it twice as high as Niagara—''

"You're pulling my leg.''

"Dead serious. They call it Virginia Falls. The whole river takes a three-hundred-eight-five-foot drop. It's quite a sight. Below the falls the river's running in a deep canyon, like your Grand Canyon.''

"That sure would be something to see.''

"There's a lot of history back in there—history and legends. The Nahanni country took a lot of lives when some of the Klondikers tried it as a shortcut to the goldfields over in the Yukon back in 1898. In 1908 a pair of brothers turned up dead up the Nahanni—minus their heads. According to the legend, the native people who lived back in there—the head-hunting Nahannies— had a white European queen. Their stronghold was a tropical valley complete with palm trees that grew right out of the permafrost.''

"Sounds like great material for a movie.''

"According to the story, there were even dinosaurs

5

back in there that lived around some steaming hot pools.''

"That's even better.'' I laughed. "Sounds like Texans have nothing on Canadians when it comes to tall tales.''

"The place where the headless prospectors were found came to be known as the Valley of Vanishing Men and then Headless Valley and finally Deadmen Valley. That was just the beginning of it. There've been lots of strange deaths and disappearances since then.''

"So what's your theory about those guys' heads?''

Clint put his finger to his dimple, then stroked his chin thoughtfully. "I figure they starved to death back in there, in late winter or spring. Bears have an uncanny sense of smell, and they come out of hibernation looking for winterkill. It's easy enough to picture bears knocking the heads loose from those skeletons, trying to get at the brains inside. After that, the skulls washed into the river or wolves carried 'em off.''

"You paint a pretty picture, Clint.''

"Listen to some of these names: the Sombre Mountains, the Funeral Range, the Headless Range, Crash Lake, Hellroaring Creek, Sunblood Mountain . . .''

"Sounds like maybe you should stay out of there.''

A grin played at his lips. "Bush pilots have a saying: 'I wish I knew where I was going to die, for I would never go near the place.' ''

Two months later, Clint would be dead—on the Nahanni. And I would watch it happen.

2

The wind blew cold across the Great Slave Lake, even at the end of August, and the first leaves were starting to fall from the birches outside my dorm room. It was still a week before school started, and the dorm was empty. I felt like I'd landed at the end of the earth, which was pretty much the case. My father was up somewhere between Yellowknife and the Arctic Ocean on a remote drill site, working seven days a week. Before long they'd be working by artificial light.

Every fourth week my father would have his time off, and that's when I'd see him. He was used to that life, from the rigs in the Gulf of Mexico and the North Sea, and he had the stamina to keep up with it. So what was I doing here? I was asking myself. How much chance was there that I was going to get to see the real North my father had been writing me about, and telling me about on his visits back to Texas? I was going to be stuck in this boarding school in the only city in the whole Northwest Territories.

I've done this to myself, I thought. Now I'm just going to be alone in a place where I don't know anybody.

I decided to get out and walk, at least see Yellow-knife. I spent a couple of days taking a good look at this boomtown that was the capital of the Northwest Territories. Yellowknife was sure-enough bustling. It looked modern—lots of steel, concrete, and glass, lots of government buildings, lots of bars.

I spotted my first moose droppings in downtown Yellowknife. They were encased in the clear plastic of a tabletop at the Mooseburger Café. They were about like a deer's, only a whole lot bigger. I thought of Clint.

I hoped I'd get some chances to see the real North-west Territories while I was up here. That's what I came for, I was telling myself. Walking around and looking at buildings had never been very high on my list. I could just imagine flying over all that wild country, like those bush pilots get to do. Unfortunately, I didn't have a bush plane at my disposal. I settled instead for holing up in my room with a Zane Grey novel about the Nava-jos. I go through a book every three or four days—westerns, mysteries, science fiction. I brought quite a few with me.

Most of the students had checked in, but I was still waiting for my roommate to arrive. This much I knew about him: he was born on the twenty-first of Decem-ber, same as me. They gave out the room assignments by pairing new kids with birthdays closest together, and you can't get much closer than being born on the same day, same year. The lady at the housing office told me that my roommate was a "Dih-nay," that it was his first year at the school, too, that his name was Raymond Providence, and that he was from a remote village.

"What's a 'Dih-nay'?" I asked her.

"It's spelled D-e-n-e," she said. "They're native people. You're probably used to calling them Indians back where you come from. They speak an Athabaskan dialect called Slavey."

I wondered if my roommate would speak much English. This was going to be interesting.

I was starting my third paperback when Raymond finally showed up, the evening before classes started. He came through the door lugging a huge duffel bag, a hockcy stick, and a bright red electric guitar. He was wearing jeans and a plaid Pendleton shirt. A little taller than me, he was a handsome kid with light brown skin and thick black hair down on his collar. He took a quick look at me, but his face was completely without expression, his dark brown eyes guarded and remote.

Now what? I thought. As he set his guitar down on his bed, I said, "Are you a rock star by any chance?"

It was a dumb thing to say; I guess I was uncomfortable. I was wondering what he was thinking about having a roommate with blue eyes and dirty blond hair. I hoped he could see I was just trying to be friendly.

"Not hardly," he said quietly, standing the hockey stick in the corner by the sink, then sitting on his bed and looking around at the confines of our room. Well, at least he speaks English, I thought. I might as well try again. Glancing at his hockey stick, I said, "I don't know much about hockey—football's the big thing where I come from. I have heard of Wayne Gretzky, though, how they call him the Great One. Are you a pretty good hockey player?"

"Pretty good, yeah."

That got a smile out of him. But even while he was smiling, his eyes stayed remote and cautious. Maybe he was a kid who'd never been away from home before. I gave him some space and went back to the book I was reading. He started unpacking.

After a while he was back sitting on the edge of his bed, looking around. I could see his eyes go to the picture over my desk, the one of my dad and me standing beside a raft down in the canyons of the Rio Grande in west Texas. "That's my dad," I said. "He's up here working."

"Oh," Raymond said. "Is he on the drilling rigs?"

"All the time. He's hoping to save up enough money so we can get some land back in Texas—we want to build a house. So how 'bout you? That's a nice-looking guitar you got there. Are you in a rock band back home?"

"Yeah, sort of."

"Maybe you can get a band together here."

"They already told me I can't play my guitar."

"You mean not in the dorm?"

"Not anywhere at this school, I guess."

"Could you switch to acoustic?"

From the look on his face, it was like I'd asked him to take up the harpsichord. I said, "They got a lot of rules and regulations here, that's for sure. I've never been in a school like this. I guess it's kind of like being in the army. So where are you from?"

"Nahanni Butte."

"Nahanni . . . ," I repeated. "Hey, I heard that name before. . . . Is it anywhere close to the Nahanni River?"

"It's right where the Nahanni River meets the Liard River."

10

"I got it now," I said. "Famous for headless men? And dinosaurs?"

He laughed. "Those headless guys must be world-famous."

I was pleased to see him relax a little.

"I never heard the part about the dinosaurs before," Raymond added with a smile. "Are you from Texas?"

"How'd you know that?"

He shrugged. "The way you talk."

"I guess I must talk funny. Sounds normal to me. I grew up in the hill country near the Guadalupe River."

"I've heard that name before, Gaudalupe River. Isn't it a little river that people float down on inner tubes?"

"How'd you ever hear that?" I asked in amazement.

"I saw it on MTV—it was a show about spring break in different places. It looked like fun—hundreds of people splashing around and all that. The water must be pretty warm."

"We used to do that all the time. It's real near where I lived. You get MTV way up here?"

"On satellite. We get thirty-nine channels."

"That's a lot more than I got back home in Texas. My grandparents don't even get cable."

"You live with your grandparents?"

"I've mostly lived with them since my mother died—almost nine years now. They're nice and all that, but it's pretty slow."

That got a laugh out of Raymond. "Man, you should try Nahanni Butte sometime if you want to talk about slow. It only has a winter road to it."

"What's that mean, 'winter road'?"

"We're about twenty kilometers away from the year-round road that they built between Fort Nelson and Fort Simpson, plus we're on the other side of the Liard River from that road. In the winter you can drive our road into Nahanni Butte because everything's frozen solid underneath, but in the summer, with all the bogs and everything, you'd just sink into the muck. It takes lots of money to put enough rock and gravel down to make a road base.''

"But they must have spent a lot of money to make a bridge across the river.''

"There's no bridge,'' Raymond said with a smile. "The Liard River always freezes real thick just up from Nahanni Butte, so it's a safe crossing there. You can drive right across the ice. They plow the snow off after every storm.''

"What about before they built your winter road?''

"When my dad was a kid, there were no roads anywhere. They had dog teams to get around in the winter. In the summer they used their boats to get in and out, on the Liard River.''

"Do you have brothers and sisters?''

"I have a younger brother and a younger sister at home, and my older sister lives with my grandmother. How 'bout you?''

"It's just me.''

Raymond didn't say anything for a while, and I thought our conversation was over. Then he looked back at me with a puzzled expression on his face and said, "I still can't believe you decided to come up here.''

"I wanted to see the North. I'd get these letters from my dad. In one of them he said there's this saying that goes, 'Once you drink from those northern waters, you'll never be happy away from them.' Have you ever heard of that saying?''

He shook his head. Raymond Providence was thinking about it, thinking about me. My roommate was wondering if I'd made a mistake.

I thought we'd hit it off real well, but the first couple of weeks it turned out Raymond and I hardly spent any time together. The native kids pretty much stuck to themselves. In the classrooms they all sat in a cluster at the back. They never spoke unless a teacher pried a few syllables out of them, and after school most of them, including Raymond, hung around together at one of the video arcades in Yellowknife. I noticed Raymond was spending most of his evenings at the library working on his math or trying to read *A Tale of Two Cities*. Once I walked over and said, "How're you doing with that book?"

"Not so good," he said.

"Same here," I told him.

"But you read all the time."

"Maybe it's a great book, but you'd have to be a walking dictionary of extinct words to read it. I think the teacher should be reading it to us, explaining everything."

Raymond had a grin on his face. "Tell him."

"He already thinks I have an attitude. He could tell I wasn't too happy when he said I couldn't do any extra-credit book reports on westerns or science fiction. They all have to be books from his list.''

After that I pretty much never saw Raymond in the library. He'd watch TV in the dorm lobby. Just before curfew he'd show up at the room, and then he'd sit at his desk and stare at his homework.

As for me, I was accepting that Raymond and I were as far apart as Texas and the Northwest Territories even though we were sharing the same room.

After school I'd been playing some pickup basketball with some of the other boom kids, making a few friends or what passed for friends. I missed playing football a lot; I missed faking out tacklers and running for daylight. I was thinking, too, about how the varsity coach back in San Antonio said I was crazy for going north when I could have such a great high school football career. The coach was practically guaranteeing me that I'd be his number one running back. He never really understood how much I wanted to be with my dad.

The third week of September was my dad's week off, and we finally got to spend some time together. It was good to be with him. The first thing he did was take me to an outdoor clothing and sporting goods warehouse to get some winter clothes for me. I've never enjoyed shopping for clothes, so I had to tell myself to be patient, because I could see this was going to take a while. We picked up a set of thermal underwear, and I decided on a pair of heavy wool trousers. My father insisted the trousers had to be wool. I was joking around, asking if he'd heard about ''the hammer,'' and he said, ''Yes indeed—the hammer's for real.''

The parka I found looked slick. It was light gray and had a waterproof outer shell and a hood ruff of genuine wolf fur. I was starting to get into this, into imagining the kind of cold that would require all this thermal over-kill. My dad recommended a thick, soft cap woven from the underfur of arctic musk-ox. I picked up a world-class pair of ski gloves and huge mittens to wear over them—everything top-of-the-line quality. "You're going to need all this stuff real soon," my dad promised.

What impressed me the most was the boots. My father got me the same kind of tall white snow boots he wore on the rigs in the winter. He pulled out the thick felt liner and said, "Gotta keep these dry, that's the key. Dry 'em out good if they ever get damp. Once they get wet, they don't insulate. You hear about people making a mistake and getting bad frostbite, even losing their feet."

Our arms were full as we stood in line at the check-out. My dad spotted a little thermometer on the display case and grabbed it. It was a couple inches long, encased in plastic. "For the zipper pull on your parka," he said.

I got a chance to try out some of the new clothes when my dad hired a charter boat the next day and we went fishing out on the Great Slave Lake. It was freezing cold out there, wind blowing, too, but I knew that was all supposed to come with the territory, and I never mentioned it. I hate whiners, so I wasn't going to be one myself. I pulled the musk-ox cap out of my daypack and warmed right up after I pulled it down over my ears.

When I caught a twenty-five-pound lake trout—a toothy predator with a head bigger than my fist—I was glad I'd come north. There was something about taking that big trout out of a body of water called the Great Slave Lake, doing it alongside my father, having him net the fish after a half hour's battle with only one of the treble hooks still attached at the last, and just barely. We were together in this strange place, and the wildness of the place itself was what had bent my rod double, and that wildness was running like electricity through the line and right through my veins. This is why I came, I thought.

We went bowling afterward, and then sat in the café at the alley and talked. With his huge hand wrapped around a coffee mug, my father talked with deep feeling about the land around the drill sites, the landscapes he was seeing from the bush planes and helicopters. Some of the sites were in the forest and some were north of the tree line, out in the barren lands. He spoke of seeing immense herds of caribou fording clear-running rivers and flowing across the tundra. He spoke of seeing a grizzly with three cubs, arctic foxes, snowshoe hares, musk-oxen. . . .

"Any wolves?"

"I keep looking. Haven't seen a wolf yet."

"So you still like it up here as much as ever?"

He had to think about that question, rubbing his beard against the grain. "Oh, I love the North, but it's a sad time to be here, to my way of thinking."

"How's that?"

"Flying into all these places where there have never been roads, knowing that the roads are coming soon, and so is everything that comes with them, for good and for bad."

"That's progress, I guess."

"It seems like everywhere the geologists have us drilling, they're finding these kimberlite pipes they're looking for, and they're finding plenty of diamonds in their core samples. It's just exploration up here now—in a couple of years the actual mines will be starting up. The talk is that the Northwest Territories could eventually rival South Africa as the world's largest diamond producer. I've worked with a couple of native people . . . they need the jobs, but they're afraid of what's going to happen. You know, they lived here for thousands of years without ruining it.''

"Isn't that because they didn't know any different?''

"I don't know. . . . Maybe it was a kind of genius, and we just can't recognize it. At any rate, it makes me sad thinking about it. You'd think we could leave the diamonds in the ground. . . . We could do without the jewelry, but we need diamond drill bits for oil and gas, and they say we even need diamonds for manufacturing those silicon chips for the computers. There's just never an end to it.''

"You could go back to the offshore rigs.''

His face brightened. ''What I'd really like to do is quit following the booms for good. Build that place in the hill country we've always been talking about. I'm gettin' far enough ahead we should be able to get a decent amount of pasture. We could raise horses.''

"Good deal,'' I said. He'd had this land dream with my mother even before I was born. ''How much longer?'' I asked.

With a smile spreading across his face, my father said, ''This winter could be it. But probably one more for insurance—the cost of land and building materials is going up all the time down there.''

"Still want to do the log house?''

"Gotta be a log house, sitting on a little bluff in some live oaks above the Guadalupe.''

"I can sure picture it.''

"You're so strong we won't even need a machine to lift the logs into place. . . . Meanwhile, I'd like to get you out some into the boondocks up here. I see a lot of great country, and you're stuck in school."

"How could we do that?" I asked.

"I'll ask my flying buddies to keep an eye out for a spot for you. I remember how much you always wanted to fly. Would you like to do some bush flying on a weekend, take a look around if they had a seat for you?"

"You know I would. I already met one bush pilot, that guy Clint who drove me from Fort Nelson. You ever fly with him?"

"No, these outfits have a lot of different pilots—how come you ask?"

"Just wondering what kind of pilot he'd make."

With daylight falling off by more than ten minutes a day and the cold attacking as we ran between classes, the dark subarctic winter was approaching, and the menace of it seemed to stretch endlessly ahead. It was early October, and homesickness was going around the boarding school like a bad virus. Though they were accustomed to the cold and the darkness, the native kids from all over Canada's North seemed to have almost no immunity to homesickness. A half dozen had already dropped out and gone home. "Dropping like flies" is how some of the boom kids put it.

I was worried about Raymond. When he looked at things, including me, he didn't really seem to be seeing them. The sadness in his eyes was unmistakable. This gray school and the gray skies were enough to dampen anyone's spirits.

I took a walk after school one day and ended up wandering inside the public rink where the school hockey team was practicing. I spotted Raymond up in the stands watching, and I joined him. We didn't say anything for quite a while, and then I asked him how it was going. He said, "Everything's too hard here. Back home, I used to be good in math. But this algebra . . . I don't get it. I don't see why they have to put letters in with the numbers."

"I know what you mean," I told him. "I had algebra last year. I thought it was going to kill me, but finally I got the hang of it. I can show you if you want."

"Could you?" he said, and I said, "Sure." We went back to watching the hockey practice. "Are these guys any good?" I asked him.

"Some of 'em are real good."

"How come you didn't go out for the team?"

"I dunno. I just like to play. At Nahanni we always just get some guys together. People come and go from the game. It's no big deal; everybody gets to play."

"Can't you just get a few guys together and come and play here on your own?"

"It's reserved for clubs and schools and stuff."

He looked awfully down to me. I said, "I still haven't even been on skates. You think you could find me a pair of skates and a hockey stick?"

"Sure, I guess. Then what?"

"Tomorrow night, let's see if we can sort of forget to leave when they close up. Maybe play some one-on-one?"

"You kidding?"

That's just what we did. As it turned out, there was enough moonlight streaming through the windows that we didn't even have to turn on the lights. Raymond was beautiful, dancing all around the ice with that puck while I was flapping around the rink like a wounded goose, laughing at myself and just trying to keep on my feet. Every time Raymond would slap the puck into the

21

net, I'd yell, "Score!" That smile never left his face the whole time, no sadness in his eyes. It was perfect. We didn't even get caught sneaking back into the dorm.

"That was way cool," he said.

"Where'd you learn to talk like that?"

"TV, I guess."

I gave him a poke. "It'll rot your mind, you know."

"You read too much. Your head will get too big."

"Then what?"

His eyebrows lifted way up and then dropped. "Explode, I guess."

After that, Raymond and I started spending more time together. I helped him with his algebra, and he was picking up on it fast. We found out there was open hockey on Sunday afternoons. I'd sit in the stands and watch him skate circles around guys. People were telling him he should be on the school team. Back in our room, I called him the Great One. I told him he'd have no trouble making the team.

He thought that was pretty funny. "Sure, Gabe. I'm Wayne Gretzky like you're a scout for the Edmonton Oilers."

"Still, you should talk to the coach—maybe it's not too late to sign up."

"Maybe next year," he said. "Tell you what—I'll go out if you go out."

"Sure, Raymond. But by the time I'm ready for the school team, you'd be ready to retire after your big career in the NHL."

Everything seemed better. I thought he was over the hump.

Right before our three-day weekend at the end of October, I got a call from Clint. He said to meet him at the floatplane dock first thing in the morning if I wanted to do some sightseeing. I realized that my father had come through for me, and I was going to get to do some flying.

Clint was saying that he hadn't heard where he was flying to yet, but he'd been hired by a Dene council to take a kid and a village elder back home. "Wear everything you have that's warm and then some," he was saying. "A polar bear would freeze to death inside that airplane!"

With the memory of my van ride with Clint not all that distant, I'd have liked it better if it had been some other pilot, but then, beggars can't be choosers.

I never had a chance to talk my flying plan over with Raymond. When I drifted off to sleep it was past curfew, and he still hadn't showed up.

In the morning I was raring to go. No guts, no glory, I told myself. Raymond had slept right through my alarm and was sleeping so soundly I didn't want to wake him up. In a couple of days, I figured, I'd be back and could tell him about my big adventure. I remembered Clint's warning and wore all my warm stuff, the thermal underwear and even the wool trousers instead of my jeans. I stuffed my daypack with a couple of changes of underwear, some spare socks, my huge mittens, and my toothbrush.

I left Raymond a note saying I was going flying, pulled on my ski gloves, and hurried through the empty streets making vapor clouds every time I exhaled. It was 7:00 A.M., an hour before first daylight. There was a good buildup of ice along the shores of Yellowknife Bay.

Clint was already there, fueling the floatplane. In a

winter flying suit with a fur ruff around the hood, he looked the part of the dashing bush pilot. "Hey, Stump," he called. "Good to see you dressed warm. Starting to cool off, eh?"

"Hammer's coming down," I agreed.

"Getting close—you'll know it when you see it. Freeze-up on the lakes and rivers is coming any day. Then the hammer. After this trip, we're switching all the planes from floats to skis."

Clint's passengers were supposed to have been ready to go at dawn. He told me about the bush plane as we waited for them. It was a red-and-white Cessna 185, single-prop, two seats in the front, two close behind, a very small cargo area behind that. Somehow I'd expected a bigger airplane. "Great old plane," Clint said. "It'll lift about anything you can stuff into it."

Dawn came and went, other planes were taking off, and Clint was muttering, "We're burning daylight." We went back inside the office, where it was warm. Clint glanced at his watch and I looked at mine.

"Hey, that's some watch you got there," Clint said. "Looks pretty high-tech."

"Bombproof, too," I said proudly. "My dad just got it for me." I fished my new pocketknife out and showed him that as well. Clint was impressed with the titanium handle. "Never seen one of these before. It's really light—much lighter than a regular pocketknife."

Ten o'clock rolled around, and still nobody had showed. Clint was muttering to himself now. We went back out to the airplane. "Too late to get there today," he said. "Can't fly in the dark—do they think this is a 747?"

"So where are we going?" I asked.

"Nahanni Butte."

I had a sinking feeling. "You said you were taking a kid home?"

"And an old man who's been in the hospital. The kid's dropping out of school."

"What school?"

"Yours. It happens all the time."

Just then I looked up and saw a slender old man with a light duffel bag coming toward the ramp. He was squinting as he took a look at the floatplane. His hair was as white as a polar bear's fur and just as thick, though not very long. His skin was a light brown. He was dressed in a cloth parka that looked homemade, and he was wearing tall moccasins that were tied with thongs at the ankle and calf.

"Here's one," Clint said. "And here comes the other."

It was Raymond, toting that big duffel bag, his hockey stick, and that red electric guitar.

Raymond's eyes took in a glimpse of me, and then they stuck on the ground. He looked embarrassed, defeated. The old man with the thick white hair looked distant and sad.

"Why didn't you tell me you were going back home?" I asked Raymond. "I had no idea."

"It didn't seem like it was any use," he muttered. "Then you would've tried to talk me into staying."

"You bet I would have! You should have told me!"

"I know. I was going to tell you this morning, but when I woke up, you were gone."

"But how come you're leaving?"

Raymond kept his eyes on the ground. I just kept waiting. Then he said, "At home I can get up when I want to, I can stay up all night if I want to, I can play hockey any time I want, I can play guitar any time I want, I can go hunting with my dad if I want to, I can mess around with my friends . . . nobody makes any rules."

"But you said it was boring back home."

Clint leaned between us and said, "I hate to rush you guys, but we're burning daylight, and daylight is

26

precious." As he grabbed their duffels, I gave him a hand with Raymond's heavy bag—everything he'd brought to school was in there. We stowed all the stuff behind the backseat, Clint arranging the load carefully around a couple of army-green metal boxes. "What's in these?" I asked.

"Those are ammo boxes," Clint replied. "Army surplus—they make good waterproof storage. We've got some food in 'em and some other survival gear."

Clint jumped back out and helped the old man into the plane through a little hatch door on the left side that gave access to the rear seats. Then Raymond climbed in. I jumped in front with Clint. I was all keyed up about my first flight ever in a bush plane. I glanced back at Raymond, wishing he was sharing in the excitement. His face had about as much expression as a wooden mask. What were people back home going to think about him dropping out of school?

Inside the airplane, doing his cockpit check, Clint seemed about ten years older than he had when he was driving the van. All business. I was feeling reassured seeing him throwing switches and pulling levers and talking over the radio while my eyes were scanning the complicated array of gauges and controls that he was reading and manipulating by second nature.

Clint told us to wear our headsets or we'd wreck our hearing, the engine was going to make such a racket. As soon as he fired it up I could see what he meant. Our headsets had mouthpieces that swung out in front of our faces. Clint switched on the intercom and started talking to us through our headsets. "Don't talk to me when I'm taking off or landing," he instructed us. "Otherwise it's fine." Then that boyish grin of his was back. He said, "Don't worry about this old ship. It's got a lot of experience—it's seven years older than I am!"

I clenched my teeth as he taxied out onto the bay. As much as I wanted to fly, I still had a knot in my stomach. I remembered my father saying once, "It's a rare bush pilot who ends up in a rest home." I had a feeling Clint was not destined for the rocking chair.

Our pilot suddenly yelled, "Let's open up the tap and pour on the coal!" With that he started his takeoff run. Water sprayed high on both sides, and with a sudden lift we were airborne.

Before long we were flying over an arm of the Great Slave Lake. Ice was showing all along the shore. Out Clint's side of the airplane I could see the open lake, vast like an inland sea. In another hour it would be noon, but the sun was pathetically low by Texas standards for the thirtieth of October.

For hours I saw mostly swampy lowlands peppered with stunted trees—not a single cabin, not a single moose. Nobody was talking over the intercom, not even Clint. Maybe we were too cold to talk among ourselves. I was flexing my toes inside the best winter boots money can buy. Raymond was hunched up against the cold and his teeth were chattering. He had his winter boots on, winter gloves, wool cap, but not enough under his parka. I couldn't tell how the old man was doing because he was seated directly behind me. I wondered why he'd been in the hospital.

At last Clint broke the long silence. "After the late start we got, we're going to have to put down in Fort Simpson for the night. We'll fly on to Nahanni Butte in the morning."

As we approached Fort Simpson on the Mackenzie

River, I took in the vastness of the Northwest Territories' biggest waterway. More than a mile wide, the Mackenzie made a spectacular sight. Scattered cakes of ice were floating in the river, and the water was reflecting the pinks and oranges of the sunset. We could see a tributary nearly as big—the Liard River—joining the Mackenzie barely upstream. It was only 4:00 P.M. when we splashed down, but day was done. The Mackenzie was headed for the Arctic Ocean, and we were headed for a couple of rooms in the tiny town above us on the bluff. In the morning we'd follow the Liard River up to Nahanni Butte.

We all ate supper together in the café. It was a pretty silent, gloomy meal, I'd have to say. I still hadn't heard a word out of the old man. Then Clint and I went to our room and watched TV. I would've rather been with Raymond, but when we checked in, Raymond had said he wanted to room with the old man from his village. Probably he didn't want me asking him more questions or trying to talk him into changing his mind. I mentioned to Clint that Raymond had been my roommate at school. Clint shrugged and said, "I guessed it was something like that. Don't feel bad about it. They drop out all the time."

Surfing the channels, Clint got all excited when he found a rodeo from the Cow Palace in San Francisco—highlights, actually, right as the show was ending. "I can't believe I missed it," he said. "You ever rodeo down in Texas?"

"Never did," I said, "but I've been thrown by a horse, if that counts."

"I'll count it," he said. "Bull ridin' was my game."

"No kidding?"

"Rode in the Calgary Stampede when I was nineteen. I was a hometown boy."

"Hey, I've heard of the Calgary Stampede."

"I'm not surprised. Calgary's big time."

"How come you gave it up?"

"For flying. Not even hockey and bull riding beat flying."

After breakfast on the last day of October, Clint fueled the airplane and we started southwest up the Liard River, which was lined with cottonwoods. Raymond was still stuck in his gloom. If he'd made a good decision, I wished he felt a little happier about it. Clint was in good spirits, which lifted mine. I'd left the boarding school behind and I was out taking a look at the Northwest Territories.

It was a sunny day, and Clint was delighted with the flying conditions. I noticed he couldn't keep his eyes off the mountains to the north and west of us.

Everywhere I could see, the forest below was crisscrossed with bulldozed paths running straight as arrows and ending on the horizon. They made a strange sight in the middle of nowhere. Clint explained that they were left over from the last boom—something to do with sonic testing for oil and gas.

Clint looked over at me, and he had a conspiratorial grin on his face. "We should go take a look at the falls on the Nahanni," he said. "Remember me telling you about it—Virginia Falls?"

"Twice as high as Niagara, right?"

"Hey, what do you guys in the back think of taking a little detour—doing some sightseeing before we take you home?" Clint asked over the intercom.

I looked over my shoulder at Raymond. He said,

30

"Whatever you want." We heard nothing from the old man.

"Raymond, have you ever seen Virginia Falls?" Clint continued.

"Never been up there."

"Never seen the canyons either?"

Raymond shook his head.

"Well then," Clint said, delighted with himself. "It's settled. We've got a perfect day for it. I'm going to give you guys a sightseeing tour you'll never forget."

With that he banked the plane to the north and west, at the same time letting out a big whoop. "Let's go find the source of the South Nahanni River! Follow it down to the falls and then all the way down to Nahanni Butte!"

"This is Cessna 6-7-Z-RAY calling Fort Simpson. Do you read? Do you read me?"

Clint let his finger off the TALK button. "I'm calling in to report our change of flight plan," he explained. "The UNICOM dispatcher must have stepped away for a minute. I'm not getting an answer."

"What's UNICOM?" I asked.

"It's for pilots flying in uncontrolled areas. Our closest one here is Fort Simpson—that's who I'm trying to raise."

The mountains were on our left now, and closer. Clint handed me a map of the Mackenzie Mountains, not a flying map but one I could read, with the rivers and the mountain ranges and all the place-names. Then he got busy with his own maps, which were all marked up with notations. He was steering west for a wide opening a river made in the front range of the mountains. "We're awful lucky today," Clint said excitedly. "There can be lots of suicide weather back here. The Mackenzie Mountains are right on the boundary between two great air masses: the cold, dry arctic air and the warm, moist Pacific air. That's why these mountains have such unstable and unpredictable weather—those two air masses are always jockeying for position.''

He reached for the TALK button again. ''This is Cessna 6-7-Z-RAY calling Fort Simpson. Do you read me?''

All we heard was some crackling static. ''We'll try again in a few minutes,'' Clint said.

I wondered if this was such a good idea, to go ahead when we weren't getting through on the radio. Nobody would know where we were going. I thought about saying something to Clint, but he was concentrating intensely on his flying. We were already starting into the mountains.

The plane took a good jolt from some turbulence, and then a few more jolts. I cinched the harness tighter across my chest. With a glance back, I saw Raymond reach over and tighten the old man's for him.

''Just a few bumps,'' Clint assured us. ''If a Chinook was blowing today, we wouldn't be doing this—we'd be looking at a fifty-mile-an-hour headwind, maybe even seventy. You see, the prevailing winds come from the west, and they can get heated by pressure and riled up by the terrain—just like water over boulders—as they come pouring down the east side of the mountains.''

Even if we weren't fighting a Chinook, I didn't feel so reassured all of a sudden. Out either side of the airplane all I could see was nearly vertical mountainsides covered with snow, timber, and rockslides. I couldn't help thinking about what would happen if the Cessna's engine quit on us. No one would even know where we went down.

Clint tried once more to get through to Fort Simpson. Again, no reply.

I said, ''Don't you have some kind of backup radio,

or some kind of emergency signaling gear besides the radio?''

"Nervous?" Clint asked with a grin.

"Heck, yes," I admitted. "Man, this is wild country."

"There's no second radio, but we do have an ELT— an Emergency Location Transmitter—fastened to the floor of the plane, just behind the partition at the rear of the cargo area."

"How does it work?"

"The impact of a crash sets it off. If we were to crash, it would start transmitting our location. It's on its own battery, and it's got a little antenna attached to it that sticks up above the airplane."

"It's good to know we have that, but what I'm wondering about is why we're not getting through to that UNICOM. You want to try again?"

"No chance of getting through now, not in this kind of terrain. We'll try again in a few minutes when we get more out in the open. Don't worry, Gabe, everything's going great, she's running like a top. Lots of times it takes a while to get through to UNICOM. That's just part of flying up here in the boonies."

I tried to relax and quit worrying. In the deep gorge below us, the river we were following wound like a snake, and Clint was all concentration adjusting to the bends. Just let him fly the plane, I told myself. Anyway, the mountainsides off both wingtips gave us no choice but to keep following this canyon upstream—no room to turn around here even if you had to. Hang on and try to think positive, I thought.

We kept following the river canyon's snaking turns until finally we cleared the pass at its headwaters and entered a world of mountains without end, ranges upon ranges, the highest ones wrapped in glaciers and cloud. I was overwhelmed by what I was seeing, thankful after all that Clint had bent the rules for me, or maybe broken them, in order to show me this. It was all too beautiful, too immense to be believed, and yet it was real. I began to read out loud some of the names from the map I was following, realizing some were names Clint had talked about the first day we met: "The Ragged Range, the Sunblood Range, the Sombre Mountains, the Funeral Range, the Headless Range . . . Hey, Clint, this is a cheerful place!"

"Up here," he replied dramatically, "nature reigns supreme."

"Listen to these! Crash Canyon, Stall Gorge, Death Lake, Hellroaring Creek . . . So where's that Deadmen Valley you had all the stories about?"

"It sits in a break down in the canyons of the South Nahanni. Up ahead here, that's the very headwaters of the South Nahanni you're looking at, right up against the N.W.T.'s border with the Yukon." He reached for the radio. "Now we'll tell 'em where we are," Clint said confidently. "Cessna 6-7-Z-RAY calling Fort Simpson. Fort Simpson, do you read? Do you read me?"

Nothing but more static.

"Could there be something wrong with our radio?" I asked.

"It was working fine this morning," he said. "But you could be right. . . . There's lots of things that can go wrong with the radio. I don't like this either, but there's nothing we can do about it right now. I'll get it checked as soon as we get back. It's no big deal, really—it's easy flying from here to Nahanni Butte."

Clint checked his watch. "It's only noon. Hey, that's why I'm hungry. Too bad we can't eat the scenery, eh?"

Behind me, the old man was tapping on one of the windows. "Caribou," Raymond explained, pointing, and then we saw them, maybe fifty caribou grazing on a windswept patch of grass atop a plateau. "Unbelievable," I whispered. I wished my dad could be seeing all this with me.

Before long we were following the Nahanni as it slipped from under the frozen ponds at its source in a wide basin ringed by peaks. "A stream flowing out of paradise," Clint purred. The river soon tumbled into a broad, forested valley flanked on both sides by mountains and more mountains. All along the way, creeks kept adding to its emerald green waters. We saw a moose along the shore, then a black bear.

This is it, I thought. The North. The Far North.

"I'm surprised there isn't more snow cover back in here," Clint commented. "There's ice all along the shore, as I'd have expected, but there's hardly any more ice running in the river than we saw in the Mackenzie. I thought it'd already be past freeze-up in the mountains. But look, the Nahanni's open all the way down through here. Probably it's been Chinooking—warm winds have melted the early snow and ice."

Up ahead, just back from the river, a huge mound of orange-and-white mineral terraces was sticking up out of the dark spruce forest. Clint headed toward it to give us a closer look. That's when we finally heard something from the old man. Suddenly he had a whole lot to say, and none of it was in English. His tone didn't sound too cheerful. I asked Raymond, "What's he saying?"

Raymond shrugged. "I've heard about that mound down there—they call it the Rabbitkettle. If the water is flowing out of the top, it's a good sign. If no water is flowing out, it's a bad sign."

Clint said with a wry grin, "I sure don't see any water coming out of that thing, do you?"

I asked Raymond, "What language was he speaking? Is that the language they speak where you're from?"

"Yeah, that's Slavey. The old people still speak it."

"I thought you did too."

"I only know a few words here and there."

"Can't he tell us in English?"

"No, he only knows a few words of English. He's my great-uncle. He was born up here somewhere on the Nahanni. I think he remembers all these places, but I bet he's never seen it from an airplane."

The sky was turning murky with high clouds racing in from the west. "A change in the weather," Clint remarked. "Probably the last day we could've done this."

A few minutes later the old man was tapping again, and pointing in the direction of the gray cliffs off his side of the airplane.

"Dall sheep," Clint said. "Gabe, see those tiny white dots way up there? The old man still has the eye of a hunter."

Up ahead, we saw the river's long calm stretch ending on a bend, where a sudden raceway of whitewater was tumbling down a gorge toward an enormous cloud of mist.

Now we could see where the whitewater was heading as it sluiced down the gorge at a steeper and steeper angle. It was racing to the edge of an immense waterfall.

"Virginia Falls!" Clint crowed. At the very brink of the drop-off, the river beat up against a towering island of solid rock that rose from the base of the falls. The island resembled a gigantic pyramid. Three-quarters of the Nahanni took its furious plunge on the pyramid's right side; the rest snaked around its back and cascaded down from the left. My eyes were mesmerized by the falling white torrents, endlessly plunging yet always remaining. Even above the plane's engine, we could hear the thundering of the falls.

I could scarcely believe the scale of what I was seeing. Clint and I exchanged glances, and he said, "Here's your payoff for coming to the N.W.T.!"

"Thanks," I told him. "Nothing could beat this." But along with the thrill, my stomach felt queasy just looking at all that relentless churning power.

Below the falls the river boiled back on itself, again and again, before it sped on its choppy way down a narrow canyon splashed with colors—orange, white, pink, and gray. According to the map, this painted canyon was the first of four canyons that started below the falls and got deeper and deeper as they went.

Raymond, who'd been born a couple hundred miles downstream from here and had never seen any of this, was studying the endless surging fury of the falls, but his face gave no hint of his feelings.

"*Na-ili Cho,*" the old man said solemnly. "*Na-ili Cho.*"

"That's the name of the falls in Slavey," Raymond explained. "They say it means Big Water Falling Down."

"Perfect on both counts," Clint agreed. "It's certainly big water, and it's definitely falling down. Virginia Falls is a terrible name for it, if you ask me. Some American came up here and named it after his daughter in the 1920s. A lot of people think they should go back to the native name.''

Clint circled the falls, giving us a revolving look from as close as he dared. Our right wingtip came within a hundred feet of the rockslides at the base of the mountain that rose out of the river—the map called it Sunblood Mountain. I turned my eyes back to the falls, noticing details like the enormous slabs of rock sticking up out of the river in the rapids above the big drop and hundreds of logs below the falls that were beached in a driftpile. Stripped of their bark and branches, as smooth as telephone poles, they spoke eloquently of the raw grinding power of thundering water.

''Do many people know about this place?'' I asked Clint. We were upstream of the falls again, over the long run of calm water that led to the rapids in the gorge and very quickly to the falls.

''Some do,'' he said, and pointed out the little dock below on the river's right shore, along the stretch of slack water. ''There's where the floatplanes tie up in the summer. Look how clear the river's running—nearly as smooth as glass. What about a pit stop?''

''You mean, land down there?''

''Sure. We can walk out along the cliffs right above the falls and take a close-up look. That's what everybody does.''

''Is there room enough to land . . . above the falls?''

With a laugh, he replied, ''All the room in the world!''

We flew around the falls for a third time, then back upstream a couple of miles before Clint swung around and landed facing downstream, holding the nose up while splashing down so gently the plane barely made a dent in the lake-like surface of the river. ''Sweet landing,'' I said. I was relieved he'd landed so far upstream, maybe half a mile above the dock.

Clint eased the throttle back. We were about a hundred feet off the right shore, taxiing slowly downstream, when suddenly the engine quit.

Inside the plane, it was eerily quiet. Not even the sound of breathing could be heard inside that airplane. The only sound to be heard was the dull roar of the falls.

Clint tried to restart the engine. "Charge on the battery's good," he muttered. "Should be starting."

I checked our speed against the trees that stood above the ragged ice lining the riverbank. We were drifting faster than I would've guessed on this flat water. All I could think of was the falls, and all I could hear was the falls and the groaning starter. Within a couple of heartbeats I went from worried to terrified. Raymond and I exchanged glances as Clint tried the starter again and again. "It could be vapor locking . . . some air in the fuel line," Clint said, thinking out loud. "Could be trouble with a screen, or maybe the fuel injectors. Could be electrical. Hang on, keep cool. . . ."

We were drifting, completely helpless, as Clint kept trying to restart the airplane. He had his left hand on the ignition switch while with his right hand he was trying to adjust two levers at the same time, one with a black knob and one with a red one. In the midst of all that he was changing the frequency on the radio and hitting the TALK button. *"Mayday! Mayday!* This is Cessna 6-7-Z-RAY at Virginia Falls on the South Nahanni River. Have landed on river, engine out, floating toward the falls. *Mayday! Mayday!* This is Cessna 6-7-Z-RAY at Virginia Falls. Engine out. *Mayday! Mayday!*''

Clint turned to me and blurted, even though I hadn't asked, ''Somebody might've heard us. We're not sure the radio's broken.''

I kept looking downstream, checking the distance that remained between us and the beginning of the gorge where the whitewater began. It was deathly quiet again inside that airplane. Suddenly Clint said, ''Gabe, remember that partition in the back of the plane right behind where we loaded the duffels. There's two canoe paddles back there. You and Raymond get out on the floats and paddle. *Paddle real hard.*''

I hesitated barely half a second, just long enough to catch a glimpse of his eyes. *''Go!''* he yelled. ''And grab the tie-rope too.''

Scrambling past Raymond and his great-uncle, I tore off my ski gloves and attacked the gear in the back, throwing it forward onto Raymond and the old man, trying to free up enough space to get at the partition and remove it. It was taking too long, way too long! All the time I was listening for the engine to catch, but all I heard was the starter laboring worse and worse as the battery weakened. I shoved the metal boxes aside, tore out the partition. I saw an ax and a rifle and a big packsack. Now I saw the canoe paddles, farther back in the narrowing tail section of the plane, taped down under some cables. I jammed myself in there and tore them out.

Raymond was waiting—he'd already removed his bulky parka. I threw mine off, then grabbed the coiled tie-rope as I climbed onto the float out the left side of the plane. While I tied the rope to the struts, Raymond crawled up to the front of the airplane and dropped out the right side onto the other float. We both knelt on one knee and started to paddle. Our strokes didn't seem to do any good.

This is impossible, I thought, but I kept digging, and Raymond matched me stroke for stroke.

The starter kept groaning, slowing, stopping. The battery had to be about dead. Maybe we'd paddled the plane a little closer to the bank, it was hard to tell. I knew the engine wasn't going to catch now. All the while the trees along the shore kept slipping by. Now we were drifting past the dock where the floatplanes tie up.

"You're gaining on it," Clint yelled from the open window of the cockpit.

He's just saying that, I thought. I kept paddling and so did Raymond. I paddled until I thought my heart would burst. Above the rumbling of the falls, I could hear the choppy sound of the whitewater racing down the gorge to the brink. With a glance downstream I saw the tree-lined riverbank ending where the cliffs of the gorge rose sheer from the river and started to climb.

We're not going to make it, I thought.

We kept paddling. I heard Raymond gasping for air; I was doing the same. It was so hard to move that airplane, and yet we'd cut the original distance to the shore by half. We still lacked forty or fifty feet. Who knew how much time was passing. It felt like forever, and it felt like no time at all. "Can you swim?" I yelled to Raymond, though I could barely manage the breath.

"Sort of," he wheezed.

"What about the old man?"

"I don't know."

With another glance downstream I saw the end of the flat water approaching, like a near horizon, and I knew we couldn't possibly get the plane to shore in time. Thirty feet remained between us and the shore. "Got to swim for it!" I yelled to Clint.

To my surprise I found Clint stepping onto the float, right beside me. He was wild-eyed, dressed only in his thermal underwear. "We need this plane and everything that's in it," he shouted. "You guys *keep* paddling and get me close, I'll tie up!" With that he grabbed the coil of tie-rope, dove into the icy water, and started sidestroking for shore. He was swimming hard. We have a chance, I thought, if he doesn't lose a stroke.

Keep paddling, I told myself, just keep paddling. But I could see the cliffs rising just downstream. The current suddenly grew stronger, much stronger. *Not going to make it,* I thought, and my mind lurched wildly in the direction of my father, trying to glimpse what this would do to him. A few seconds later I felt the airplane tilt as it dropped into the first whitewater riffles. It felt like we were starting down a slide.

I looked up and saw Clint struggling onto the ice along the shore, crawling on his knees. At last he was up on his feet and snubbing the rope around the only tree within reach. Too late? The plane was already into the first choppy waves of the rapids. I caught a glimpse of Raymond's face, the whites of his eyes: he knew we were dead. He was looking downstream into the thundering maw of the rapids, where whitewater poured between ledges, surged into deep holes, and boiled against enormous slabs of rock.

It was then I felt the tie-rope go taut and seize the airplane. I was jerked off balance and lost my paddle, but I managed to cling to the struts as the plane swung like a pendulum against the shore under the cliff at the beginning of the gorge.

In another moment Clint was there, along an icy ledge, helping me and Raymond and the old man to safety. The next moment Clint was inside the airplane handing things out to us as fast as he could, from me to Raymond to the old man: parkas, gloves, duffel bags, my daypack . . . Here came the metal boxes, the pack-sack, the ax, the rifle, even the hockey stick and the electric guitar.

"Thank God we're all safe," exclaimed Clint as he regained the safety of the shore. We grabbed whatever gear we could carry and worked it up the ledge to the bank. We made a second and then a third run. The old man was surprisingly nimble on the ice. The rope to the plane was as taut as a bowstring and seemed as if it might break at any second. Clint said, "The airplane's in an awful lot of current—I'm afraid we're going to lose it. We've got to try to get another rope on it, find something else to tie to—"

"Do we have another rope?" I yelled, looking around. I sure didn't see one.

"Look in that packsack by your foot," Clint hollered back. I pulled a tentbag out of it, saw two sleeping bags in stuff sacks, a red wool blanket. "No rope," I reported. Clint didn't know it, but he was so cold after being in the river that his skin had turned purple. The wind started blowing hard, and it was cold, cold. Raymond and I pulled on our parkas and our gloves. "Get some clothes on!'' I said to Clint, but he ignored me. His eyes were on that rope and he was trying to think.

Clint was right—the rope was going to break, maybe real soon. I thought about what might still be on the plane that we needed. ''The emergency transmitter!'' I yelled. ''Can you get it off the plane?''

''It's built into the plane, like I told you,'' he yelled back, but he was thinking about it, I could tell. He said, ''I might be able to get back in there and activate the switch. . . .''

Clint stared at the rope, then at the plane. Suddenly he looked up and gasped, ''My God, the box of rifle shells . . . it's still on the plane, under my seat. I've got to try to get back on the plane!''

''The rope, Clint,'' I yelled. ''Look at the rope!''

''We need those shells!'' he shouted, and skittered back down the ledge, stepped to the float, and disappeared inside the airplane. I followed him down the shore in case I could help.

Suddenly, with a loud cracking sound, the spruce tree that Clint had tied to broke loose at the roots. It wasn't the rope that broke, it was the tree. Raymond and the old man were clear of it, but that stubby tree was shooting my way, and I could see I was going to get brushed right off the ledge and into the river. I reached for the packsack at my feet, then timed my leap as best I could. The tree passed under me, most of it—a branch tripped me up, and I fell hard. I swung around and saw the tentbag go into the river. Then I looked up and saw the tree sloshing through the waves, and out beyond it, the airplane already well downstream, with Clint standing there on the float and looking back at me. ''Gabe, catch!'' he yelled.

Clint tried to heave the box of ammunition to me, but he was already too far away and the box landed way short. "Clint!" I hollered back, but there was nothing to tell him to do. I stood frozen in place, utterly helpless.

Over the roar of the whitewater, I heard him shout, "Sorry!" He kept looking back at us as the Cessna wallowed into the first hole and came out upright. So far he was still hanging on, still looking back.

Clint never tried to swim for it. On both sides of the river down there it was nothing but sheer cliffs, with huge whitewater wall-to-wall in between. Clint clung to the struts, trying to ride it through as long as possible. I saw him lift his cap and wave it with his free hand while he hung on one-handed. Like he was riding a bull, I realized. Then I heard him whoop as the plane rose up onto the first of two roller-coaster waves.

Miraculously, the airplane was staying upright. But just before the rapids bent out of sight and raced down to the brink of the falls, the plane was swept against a boulder jutting out of the river. The Cessna crumpled like a toy, tipped over, and was swept away. I saw only the briefest glimpse of Clint being pitched into the whitewater, and then he was gone. "Clint!" I yelled. "Clint!"

Raymond and I ran up the steep footpath along the rising rim of the gorge. We stopped at a bend in the cliffs and looked down to the brink of the falls. We saw nothing but an insanely tilted river plunging toward the brink, where it was all mist and roar and thunder. "Could he survive that?" I asked Raymond.

"I don't see how," Raymond said.

I felt as if every nerve in my body had just been cut with a knife, as if what had just happened to Clint had

47

happened to me. I said, "I don't think he could be alive either, but we need to go down below the falls and look." My mind was racing, my heart pounding so loud I could hear it. He must have family back in Calgary, I thought.

"It'll be dark soon," Raymond said. "It must be after three already."

"You're right," I told him, checking my watch.

"There's probably a flashlight in all that stuff that came off the airplane. You go down and look for him. I'll try to bring a flashlight so we can find our way back."

Raymond took off running, and I headed into the forest to stay well clear of the cracks in the rim of the gorge. When I was opposite the falls itself, I came out onto the ledges and looked down into the raging sheets of water, the roar and the foam and the spray. I could feel the solid rock below my feet vibrating like a tuning fork. As it ran up through me I felt my whole body vibrating with fear. Downstream in the painted canyon there was no sign of the airplane, but it was hard to see down there through the mist, and the day was dimming down so fast. I imagined Clint holding his breath, tucking himself into a ball, somehow pulling himself up onto the beach right below the falls where I couldn't see. But I knew I was thinking pure fantasy.

Back in the woods, I stumbled around in the frozen mosses until I found the footpath again. It led in switchbacks down a steep slope to the river below the falls. Above the ice lining the shore it was all rubble down there, nothing but river rocks coated with transparent ice and the driftpiles of slick logs I'd seen from the air. I worked my way upstream toward the falls, which now loomed right in front of me. I kept concentrating, trying to spot the red-and-white colors of the airplane.

I kept thinking I'd somehow find Clint alive on the shore. But I knew that really I was looking for a body. I slipped and crawled the rest of the way to the falls, as close as I could get, where the thunder deafened me and the spray made the water run down the shell of my parka. Nothing. Not a trace of Clint or the airplane, only the endless boiling of the river back on itself before it raced downstream. It was getting dark. Numb, I turned back, slipping on the rocks. I saw a flashlight coming down the last few switchbacks from above. "Find any thing?" Raymond called.

"Nothing," I called back.

When we met at the foot of the slope, I said, "What now? What about us? What's going to happen to us?"

"All I know is, we got to make a fire and we got to do it quick." Raymond was shivering uncontrollably. "You won't believe how cold it's going to get," he added.

He turned and started walking up the trail on the steep switchbacks. I followed, trying to keep close to his light. "Do you think somebody might have heard Clint's Mayday?"

"Could have," Raymond said doubtfully.

"Well, if his Mayday didn't get through, then we have to hope that the emergency transmitter he told us about is working. Maybe he got it turned on. Maybe hitting those rocks set it off. . . ."

"Are you kidding?" Raymond said, stopping to look at me in disbelief. "The whole thing's underwater— look at this falls! Don't you remember what he said about how it works, the antenna and all? The plane would've busted up and got smashed over and over against the bottom of the river. That antenna would've got broken off. This river, it chews everything up.''

"Maybe it worked for a minute or two,'' I said, grasping at straws.

"Maybe.'' Raymond shrugged, and started up the trail again. Over his shoulder, he said, "If somebody heard the Mayday, or if the transmitter worked, we'll know in a day or two. They'll rescue us real quick.''

My heart was beating so fast I was afraid I was having a heart attack. I steadied myself against a big rock along the trail. "Wait up,'' I called, trying to catch my breath. "People will know we're missing. My dad, your parents . . . Who searches for missing planes?''

"The Royal Canadian Air Force and the bush pilots.''

"How much do they search?''

"A lot. Tomorrow we can get a real smoky signal fire going.''

"Do we have any food?''

"I didn't have time to look. Let's go find out.''

"Man, it's getting cold,'' I said. "This must be the arctic air that Clint was talking about.'' I stumbled on a root and went down hard. I picked myself back up. "I can't believe this happened,'' I mumbled, catching up. "We're in a world of trouble, Raymond.''

"You got that right.''

8

The old man already had a fire going. It brought us in like a beacon. We huddled close, absorbing the heat. I kept picturing the airplane breaking up, Clint disappearing in the whitewater. Then I was back on the float, paddling as hard as I could but never getting any closer to the shore. My mind wouldn't let go of the pictures.

The old man was sawing firewood with a folding bow saw. It seemed odd how unhurriedly he was working, just as if he was on a camp-out. Back from the fire, ten feet or so, he'd already built a lean-to of spruce boughs floored with a deep layer of boughs and tips.

"Don't get the front of your boots too close to the fire," Raymond warned.

I took a step back.

"It's a good thing he's with us," Raymond said.

"Who?" I asked, still in a daze.

"Him," Raymond said, pointing with his face toward the old man. "Those old guys like him . . ."

"What's his name?"

"Johnny Raven."

Hearing his name, the old man looked up. He'd set

the bow saw aside and was digging through one of the waterproof army boxes. He fished out some tea bags and handed Raymond a big aluminum pot that had a second one nested inside, motioning with the pots toward the river. "He wants me to get some water," Raymond told me.

"I'll go with you," I said.

The thunder from the falls grew louder as we came over a little rise. I said, "I still can't believe this really happened."

"Me either. It's bad."

We were approaching the river. The whitewater sounded close. Suddenly Raymond's flashlight beam fell on the freshly broken roots of the spruce tree Clint had tied to. Raymond said, "He should never have flown us way back up here. He'd still be alive if he'd done what he was supposed to do—just taken us home."

"I know," I agreed. "He was like a little kid, all excited about flying. I think he was a good pilot; he just had bad luck. It wasn't really his fault about the engine quitting."

"Could've been it was his fault, the way it conked out. Who knows? And what about the radio? He shouldn't have kept going. People always say about the bush pilots, Bad luck can happen to anyone, but you can't afford to make stupid mistakes."

Raymond took the aluminum pots apart to get the water. "Here," I said. "Let me hold the light." I flashed it along the shore. The ice had grown considerably in the last few hours. "Man, it's cold," I said.

"Tell me about it."

"Let me give you a hand so you don't slip. Careful . . ." My mind kept racing. "If the Mayday didn't get through," I said, thinking aloud, "and the emergency transmitter got wrecked . . . What I'm trying to figure out is, where are they going to be searching for us?"

"Along the Liard River, where we were supposed to be."

"That's what I was afraid of."

"I know."

Raymond was way ahead of me, I realized. "How much food could there be in those metal boxes?"

"Not much, I guess."

We brought the water back to the old man, and he brewed tea. It felt good to get something hot inside our bodies. The old man had fished out the sleeping bags for us and wrapped himself in the red wool blanket. He looked calm in the light of the fire. I felt anything but calm.

Raymond was looking into one of the metal boxes with the flashlight. "Any food in there?" I asked.

"Some," he said. "A sack of flour, a can of baking powder, a box of salt—we can make bannock. Big bag of beans, about five macaroni-and-cheese dinners, some boxes of dried fruit."

"That's it?"

"That's it."

Now Raymond was going through his duffel bag and pulling out clothes, laying them on a blue vinyl tarp he'd pulled out of the second army box. His three pairs of gym shoes looked as out of place as his electric guitar and the hockey stick propped up against the tree behind him. "Lucky I have all these clothes with me," he said, as he unlaced his boots and stepped onto the tarp, quickly stripping down to bare flesh and reaching for his thermal underwear. "What do you have in your daypack?"

"A couple of changes of underwear, some heavy winter socks, a wool scarf, my big mittens. I'm wearing my thermals, a heavy wool shirt, and I've got these heavy wool trousers."

"Not enough," he said, and handed me a sweater, then another one to the old man. "I got two more pairs of trousers, one for you and one for me."

"You mean wear two pairs at the same time?"

"That's what he's doing already," Raymond said, nodding toward his great-uncle.

"What about his feet in those moccasins?"

"Those big moosehide moccasins work as long as they're dry. Those old guys like him are tough."

"What about your boots? They don't look as good as mine."

"Good enough," Raymond said. "They're new, too. My dad got 'em for me when he took me to Yellowknife." Raymond took a turquoise ski headband out of the pocket of his parka and handed it to the old man, who didn't seem to have a cap. The old man said something in his language and pulled the headband over his ears. He didn't look tough to me. He looked frail.

Raymond and I crawled into the shelter with our sleeping bags and started arranging them on the spruce boughs. The old man was still sitting by the fire, wrapped in the blanket. Raymond said, "Sleep in everything you got on; you're going to need it."

"In Scouts," I said, "when I was a kid . . . they told us it was warmer to sleep nude inside your sleeping bag."

"Ha! I wish I could tell that to Johnny! He'd think that was pretty funny. Want to try it tonight?"

"No thanks," I said. "I think I'll take your advice. All I'm taking off is my boots."

Within two minutes there was a little whistle in Raymond's breath. He was already asleep. I bent double against the cold and watched the full moon rise over the mountains through a break in the clouds. I was shivering, more from fear, I think, than from the cold. The adrenaline was still pumping panic through my veins. Try to be brave, I told myself. This is when it really counts. I could hear my mother telling me how strong I was, how tough. She always said that. I didn't feel strong at all. I felt more like crying.

A branch was sticking me in the side. I tossed and turned, realizing how hungry I was. Tomorrow we'd eat something. Not much, that's for sure. I wasn't going to mention food again. And no more complaining about the cold, I told myself. That's not going to make it any warmer. No matter what happens now, at least I'm not alone. I have Raymond and that old man Johnny Raven. I drifted off thinking about my father. By now he knows we're missing. He'll make sure they keep searching until they find us.

I woke in the dim twilight of morning to a crackling sound. I didn't know where I was. All I could see was Raymond's black hair sticking out of the zippered top of his sleeping bag. I smelled the pithy scent of spruce trees. Then it all came back, what had happened and where we were. The crackling sound was the sound of the campfire. And now I saw that three inches of snow as fine as salt had fallen during the night. It was bitter cold. I heard the background roar of the falls and remembered Clint and all that talk about the hammer. Well, I thought, the hammer's down now, no question about it. I looked at my watch. It was just before 8:00 A.M., and the date said it was the first day of November.

Raymond kept sleeping. I joined the old man at the campfire. He acknowledged me with a nod of his head and a gentle smile. The old Dene was still wrapped in the wool blanket. The years had worn his face with so many creases it looked like a map of all the rivers and streams in the North. With a twist of his lips, he pointed to a bannock he'd evidently just taken out of the frying pan. He'd set it aside to cool on his woodpile, and it was still giving off heat. The old man got up and tore off a big piece for me, taking a very small one for himself. I took off one mitten and accepted it from his hand. It was warm and delicious, the first food I'd eaten since our breakfast at Fort Simpson. "Good," he said in English.

"Good is right," I agreed. "The bread of the North. We had bannock at the boarding school. At first I thought it was a pan pizza without anything on it."

I could see he liked it that I was talking to him even though he couldn't understand much.

I slipped my mitten back on and walked over to the river. I stood there staring at the hole in the ground, looking again at the broken roots where the spruce had stood. From the hanging shelves of ice along the shore, I could tell that the river had dropped two or three feet overnight. The Nahanni looked so different from the day before that I was stunned. Today it was filled with hissing cakes of mush ice, and the sky was filled with gray clouds and snow. The snow was falling on the rocky slopes of Sunblood Mountain, which rose from its immense base along the opposite shore. I remembered the little thermometer attached to the parka's zipper pull at my neck. I zipped it down far enough to read what it said. Twenty-two degrees below zero. The coldest I'd ever seen in my life was twenty-four above. They'd better find us soon, I thought.

When I returned to the fire, Raymond was there eating his bannock. I could see he wasn't going to have much to say, and I didn't blame him. The old man handed me a cup of hot tea. A half-dozen gray jays showed up out of nowhere and snatched the crumbs from around Raymond's feet. "We call that bird 'camprobber,' " he said.

"You should see the river this morning," I said. "It's full of ice."

"Gonna freeze up now. November is winter. But I thought of something else about our chances for getting rescued."

"What is it?"

"There's a few hunting cabins along the Liard River. They call that part the Long Reach. People are still hunting moose down there now. Somebody could have seen our plane go away from the river, toward the mountains."

"Now you're talking," I said.

"Then they wouldn't spend all their time looking up and down the river. They'll come looking in the mountains."

"And maybe they'll figure out we wanted to go see the falls! We'll get a smoky fire going today, like you said. We'll be out of here!"

The old man was making an inventory of all the emergency gear from the plane, laying everything out on the blue tarp for us to see. He was pleased with each and every item: a few pots and pans, a few utensils, two plastic water bottles, a sheath knife, a slim bone-handled knife Raymond said was a skinning knife, a folding camp shovel, a whetstone and file, the bow saw and two spare blades, the ax, and the useless rifle. Old Johnny Raven checked the rifle's tubular magazine for shells and found it empty, pulled the bolt back and exposed the chamber, and was disappointed to find the chamber empty too.

Raymond was arranging a number of smaller items. He set out three packs of parachute cord a hundred feet long each, a first-aid kit, a compass, a sewing kit, a small fishing tackle box, a pencil and notepad, four candles, and a cigar box with two butane lighters and a box of kitchen matches inside.

There was one other item that Raymond had picked up and was turning over in his hands, trying to figure out what it was—a fluorescent-orange plastic case about four inches long. Raymond pulled it apart, and a white cube fell out onto the ground. A round metal dowel stuck out of the handgrip of the device, and a short flat bar stuck out of the cap piece. I glanced at the old man; he was keenly interested.

"I think it's a fire starter," Raymond said, scraping the flat striker against the metal dowel and producing a heavy shower of sparks, which greatly impressed the old man and both of us as well. Raymond showered the white cube with sparks. Nothing happened. Nine, ten times he tried, but nothing happened. "I guess it doesn't work," I said.

Old Johnny Raven took out his pocket knife and scraped the top of the cube a little. It had the consistency of soap. He made a few little shavings on the top surface of the cube, then set the cube back on the ground carefully so the shavings would stay in place.

This time Raymond's first shower of sparks set the cube aflame. Johnny Raven's eyes went wide and so did ours. The flame rose to a height of about five inches. The old man snatched up a handful of snow and smothered the flame, retrieved the cube, and set it on his palm admiringly. I borrowed the cube and took a sniff of it. "Some kind of petroleum product," I reported to Raymond. The old man inserted the cube back into the case, which he snapped shut. Then he cut a length of parachute cord and hung the fire starter around Raymond's neck. Raymond stuffed it inside his parka. "We'll only use it if we have to," he said.

As soon as our inventory was done, the old man had us pack everything up. Evidently he wanted us to leave this spot. It took quite a bit of doing for him to explain himself, since he had so few English words and Raymond had so few Slavey. Johnny Raven wanted us to move upriver. The day was gray, windy, and bitter cold, and we had a good fire going, so we didn't get too excited about the idea. Finally, by acting out an elaborate pantomime, the old man made us understand that there was plenty of dead wood upstream for firewood and very little here. "I should've known that," Raymond said. "I just didn't think. Green spruce like we have here is hard to get to burn. You need a lot of dead wood to get it to burn at all. And we need to make a big fire, for the search planes."

We lugged everything up to the new camp, on a rise above a small creek a couple hundred feet back from the Nahanni. The creek was almost completely frozen over. At the edge of a stand of dead timber Raymond and I started our signal fire. We built it up big and threw on a couple of rotten logs to make plenty of smoke.

We stood back and watched the smoke rise high in the sky. Raymond said, "We have to keep this fire burning good every day in case they're looking anywhere near here."

I said, "I keep thinking about what you said this morning . . . how somebody might have seen our plane turn away from the river, toward the mountains. I keep thinking, what if nobody saw that? Then what? They'll just keep searching up and down the Liard, right? What's it like along there? All forest, isn't it?"

"That's right—like you saw. Cottonwood trees along the river, spruce everywhere else."

"Hard to see a plane in a thick forest like that, right? So they'll keep searching over and over, thinking they'll eventually find the plane hidden down in the trees somewhere."

"I guess so."

"Or they could think the plane must have gone down in the river, and that's why they can't find it. It could've sunk."

Raymond shrugged.

"I'm just trying to think," I said. "If they don't show up soon, I guess we just have to hang on here until they widen the search and start looking way up in the mountains. I hope the weather back here doesn't get too bad for flying."

When we returned to the new campsite, the old man took the ax from us and quickly fashioned three long poles from skinny spruce trees, then lashed them together near their tops with a piece of parachute cord.

Now he stood them up, making a tripod. Taking the folding camp shovel from one of the army boxes, he peeled a big piece of frozen moss from the ground and gestured that he'd like Raymond to produce a whole lot more of the same. Assembling the bow saw into its triangle shape, he showed me he wanted green spruce boughs and plenty of them. A few seconds later he was back to cutting more poles.

"What are we making here?" I asked Raymond.

"I've never seen one before, but I've seen pictures. I think he's building a brush teepee, like they used to live in during the winter in the old days when people lived out in the bush."

"What do you usually sleep in when you're out camping in the winter?"

He laughed. "I've slept outside in the winter two nights in my whole life, and one of 'em was last night. On my dad's trapline he has tiny cabins all along the way. Once we got caught by a storm, and my dad had to build one of those lean-tos like Johnny made last night. But this brush teepee's going to be a lot warmer. They lived in these. They built fires in them and everything."

The day was already dimming. The actual daylight had come and gone so fast. This far north, I realized, winter days are going to be mostly twilight. We were all moving quickly, without a word being spoken. It wasn't long before we were patching the brush teepee together over the bare spot Raymond had cleared. Into the forks of the tripod we placed all the poles the old man had cut, then laid on layers of moss and boughs. Johnny Raven wanted us to leave the very top open

61

where the poles crossed. "That's for the smoke to get out," Raymond explained.

We chinked the shelter with moss as tight as we could, leaving an opening between two poles for a small entrance. Except for the fire ring in the middle of the shelter, we lined the floor with boughs and tips, three or four inches thick. It was already apparent that this night would be colder than the last. We used the rest of the twilight to make a small pile of split firewood and bring it inside.

The old man, in constant motion, went to the creek and chopped a hole in the ice for water. Gone was the sad expression I'd seen on his face at the floatdock at Yellowknife Bay. He seemed perfectly content.

We cooked up one of the macaroni-and-cheese dinners. I could've eaten ten times that much and a bucket of fried chicken besides. It was smoky in there; the smoke found its way directly up and out of the shelter only some of the time. Mostly we had to keep low, where the air was good. I ate lying down, propped on one elbow.

That night I woke to the howling of wolves. I knew immediately that's what they were. When my dad and I had heard the yipping and singing of coyotes out in Big Bend National Park along the Rio Grande, it had seemed an eerie curiosity. The howling of these wolves was deeper, more sustained, somber and ghostly. It distilled all my fears of the cold, the darkness, and the unknown, and I felt the hackles rising on the back of my neck. I was grateful we weren't out in the open. I remembered how my dad had always wanted to see a wolf.

I lay back down. After a few minutes the wolves quit,

but I couldn't go back to sleep. Later I heard something snuffling around, brushing against the shelter. A bear, I was sure of it. This time I flicked the flashlight on and gave Raymond a poke. "A bear," I whispered.

Raymond listened. "Maybe so," he agreed.

Wrapped in his blanket, Johnny Raven motioned for the flashlight. Taking the ax with him, he parted the boughs at the entrance and slipped outside. A few seconds later we heard two dull thuds. He came back inside. "Porky-pine," he announced softly.

In the morning Johnny Raven built a larger fire outside the brush teepee and placed the porcupine on the fire. When most of the quills and fur had melted, he pounded the rest off with a stick. After the porcupine cooled, he gutted it, but he let us know that the charred skin should be left on. He set some big pieces on to boil. The meat was full of fat. Under the circumstances, it looked okay to me. I would've tried anything that resembled food.

The porcupine meat tasted something like pork, only richer. As we filled our stomachs, Raymond said, "My father used to say that the porcupine knows the land so well that the lines in the palm of its hand are actually a map of all the places it goes." I looked at the old man eating with great satisfaction, and I thought that the hairs on his chin looked just about like two or three dozen stubby porcupine quills. I got the crazy image in my head that he was half porcupine.

We built up the signal fire, made it smoke, and stood back and watched. "Man, we could use that airplane about now," I said. I knew that if no plane showed up today, it meant they weren't coming anytime soon.

Raymond hadn't even heard me. He'd walked off a little, and was looking at something on the ground. Droppings. "There's a moose around here, maybe not far away," Raymond said. "These aren't very old."

"I'll bet Johnny knows ways of killing a moose even without using a rifle," I said. "Maybe we can get by without those shells. Can't he make a bow and arrow or something?"

Raymond gave it some thought. "I've never seen anybody doing that, or heard about it. . . . Even the old guys have always had rifles."

"Maybe we can live off porcupines," I said hopefully. "It didn't taste so bad."

Raymond chuckled. "So you liked that porcupine, eh? Good idea, but you don't see that many porcupines. Rabbits maybe. Some years there's a lot of rabbits in the winter."

We felled a half-dozen more trees for firewood while the old man collected rose hips for tea, from the wild rosebushes along the creek. His little pot of bright red rose hips reminded me of my mother, who used to love rose hip tea. Raymond and I sawed our firewood timber into ten-foot lengths and dragged it to camp. Then we took turns with the saw, making rounds about eighteen inches long to be split for the small fire inside the shelter.

Working kept us warm. A few minutes of inactivity, and the cold started to seep in, especially through our gloves. As bundled up as I was, stomping around the snow in my huge boots, I felt like some inflated version of myself and nearly as awkward as an astronaut on the moon.

We kept watching the sky and listening for the sound

65

of an airplane. The vapor from our breathing made bursts of cloud every time we exhaled or spoke. I noticed that the stiff wolf hairs on my parka ruff would barely start to collect frost before they shook it loose. No frost at all was forming on the dark fur ringing Raymond's parka hood. I asked him what kind of fur it was, and he said, "Wolverine."

We went to take a look at the river. Twilight was on us already. All the cakes of ice were expanding and adhering, slowing down and growing into a solid mass. The river was freezing shut before our very eyes. I tried not to think ahead, not to let myself think about slowly starving to death in this place, but I couldn't help it.

"Nobody's coming today," I said softly. "It's already getting dark."

"Nobody saw the plane turn away," Raymond said conclusively. "They would've been here by now."

"I know," I agreed. "Nobody heard any Mayday or the transmitter either."

We walked back up together to the signal fire, and stared into the flames for a long time. There was nothing more to say.

The next morning we were eating beans for breakfast, and old Johnny Raven was inspecting the little fishing tackle box. I thought how useless the shiny lures would be with the river frozen. Johnny lifted up the little tray on top to get a look at what was underneath, and he let out a sudden cry. He held up a long rifle shell, then three more. The old man jumped up and made a beeline for the rifle hanging in the tree. He pulled the bolt back and tried a shell in the chamber. The face of the old hunter showed clearly that the ammunition made a match with the rifle. "Per-fec," he said. He ejected the shell from the chamber, then slid all four into the rifle's tubular magazine.

Raymond's face was all lit up. "We have a chance now," he said. "If Johnny gets a moose, we can hold out until they find us."

I took a good look at the old man cradling the rifle in his arms. There was a glint in his eye now. I thought, I sure hope you're a good hunter.

A moment later Johnny was showing us what else was in the bottom of the tackle box: ten or twelve more of those white cubes to replace the one in the fire starter around Raymond's neck. "Good deal," Raymond said softly, patting the old man on his shoulder. "Good going, Johnny."

The old man proceeded to sharpen the ax with the file, then the sheath knife and the skinning knife with the whetstone. He didn't seem in any hurry. I said, "Any time he wants to go get a moose, that would be okay by me."

"Those old guys never say they're going hunting," Raymond said. "Even my father, he never says he's going hunting. It's bad luck. They just say they're going for a walk. They think that way the animals won't overhear them. Sometimes they'll say, 'I'm going out to see if I can find a moose track,' or even 'I'm going out hunting for nothing.' "

Just after noon Johnny spoke quietly in Slavey to Raymond, who nodded his head to indicate he understood his intent if not his exact words. The old man slipped out of camp with the rifle over his shoulder and disappeared upriver.

"Think he'll get something?" I asked.

"Johnny's got a lot of luck," Raymond replied. "He always gets one."

"He should get a couple. I could take care of one myself."

"If he gets a moose, he can make snowshoes," Raymond said. "He'll make the frames from birch and everything else from babiche."

"What's that?"

"I think you call it rawhide."

"With snowshoes, we could walk out of here if we had to," I said.

Raymond shook his head. "I don't know if that's possible, with all the mountains and canyons and everything. And we'd have to leave our signal fire to try it."

"I didn't think of that," I admitted. "You're right, we have to stay right where we are. They'll search in wider and wider circles. Someday they'll fly right over here. Like I said, my dad'll turn over every rock. He's probably hired his own plane. I'm sure of it. That's what he'd do—he'd never give up."

Johnny's face looked haggard as he walked into the firelight in the early darkness. We didn't have to ask if he'd had any luck. "It can take a long time to get a moose," Raymond said.

That night the Nahanni froze solid as iron. A couple of days after that, Raymond and I were surprised to suddenly see a moose with her calf cross on the ice a few hundred yards upriver, but Johnny was away hunting and there was nothing we could do but stand and watch them. I'd known moose were big animals, but I hadn't imagined how big. It looked to me like the mother could've stood six feet at her shoulders. With their huge, drooping noses and big ears, they looked

68

vaguely like mules. We were rationing our food so closely now, one tiny meal a day in the morning, it hurt to see all that meat on the hoof just walk away.

Every day, while Johnny was out hunting, we kept our signal fire going big and smokey. Like me, Raymond was always looking to the sky, always straining to hear the sound of a motor. We'd quit talking about rescue planes or the big "what if" that we both had on our minds: What if a plane never comes? We were just living day to day.

The old man never slowed down. In camp he broke the ice in the creek and hauled water, he cut inner soles from the red blanket to add some more insulation to the wool felt lining of his moccasins, and he did the same for Raymond's boots. He showed us where to find cranberries. They were frozen, of course, but still clinging to the bushes. By themselves they tasted pretty tart, but were delicious baked into the bannock.

On the eighth of November we woke up to snow— a dry, stinging snow that was piling up fast. The morning stayed dark. As usual, I had slept only in fits. I let myself think about my hunger. I let myself imagine being trapped here in deeper and deeper snow. Suicide weather, I thought. No search planes today, that was for sure. We watched as Johnny picked up the rifle and waded off in the snow. I knew he wasn't going to find a moose. Raymond wasn't saying anything. He just stayed in the brush teepee, fed the fire, and waited.

I couldn't stand the waiting, and I hated being pinned down. I walked around out in the snow a little—there was nowhere to go, nothing to do. I went back inside and said to Raymond, "We got to think of something else."

He looked up at me. "Like what?"

"I don't know what," I said, giving in to my frustration. "I just don't think Johnny's going to get a moose, and we're watching the days go by."

"It takes a lot of work to get a moose sometimes," Raymond said slowly. "And you have to be lucky— that's what they always say. But it'll be easier now to track them in the snow."

I could picture that. I could picture Johnny following tracks in the snow. My paranoia backed off a few notches. "I didn't think of that," I admitted.

The weather cleared overnight. The mountains all around were cloaked with snow. We spent the days straining to hear the sound of the airplane that never came, hearing nothing but the profound stillness of the northern forest. I suggested to Raymond that maybe he should be the one trying to get the moose. He dismissed the idea. "I've been out with my father some—I even got a moose once," he said. "I can hunt, but not like those old guys. A moose can hear the snap of a twig from way far off, and they can smell a man from a couple of miles. I might get one if I was real lucky, but I'd probably waste bullets. Have you ever hunted?"

"My dad was always away during deer season, so I never had a chance."

Right while we were talking, a couple of caribou ran by—definitely within the range of a rifle. But of course we didn't have the rifle. The caribou were in such a big hurry we weren't even sure they saw us. Going somewhere where there's something to eat, I thought. I felt more light-headed than ever, and unsteady on my feet. "What else is around besides moose and caribou?" I asked impatiently.

70

"Dall sheep," Raymond answered, "but they keep up in the cliffs where wolves can't go. There's black bears, but they probably went into their dens when this cold weather started. They usually den about the end of October. Johnny will be keeping his eye out for a den entrance. If he finds one, he'll hunt it in its den."

"People really do that?"

"All the time. They watch carefully in the fall for signs that a bear's making a den. Sometimes the bears tear out blueberry plants for bedding. When a hunter finds a den, he'll wait until the middle of the winter to go get the bear."

"What about grizzlies?"

Raymond looked uncomfortable that I'd even brought up the subject. "They say grizzlies den a few weeks later than black bears. They live back in the mountains."

"But that's where we are," I pointed out to him.

He ignored my remark. "Black bears are what's good to hunt," he continued. "Grizzlies aren't supposed to taste so good. One of the Slavey names for grizzly is supposed to mean 'keep out of its way.' "

The following day the weather suddenly changed. A warm wind came ripping down off the mountainsides at midday and melted all the snow. The thermometer on my parka zipper read fifty degrees *above* zero. I even pulled off my gloves and my fur cap. The Fahrenheit reading didn't mean much to Raymond, but fortunately my little thermometer had the Celsius scale on it, too, and he was impressed when he heard it was ten degrees Celsius. "It's the Chinook," Raymond said. "It's back."

71

"It's unreal," I said. "Such a big temperature swing so fast. I thought the hammer was down for good."

"Chinooks come and go in the early winter."

"I'm not complaining," I assured him. "Keep it coming. It sure beats the cold."

The warm winds blew day and night. In a couple of days the Nahanni broke through its ice, smoking where it hit the air. Great blocks of ice jostled their way downstream among the hissing floes of mush ice. Before long the river had opened a wide channel of water flowing toward the falls.

In the morning the Chinook was blowing stronger than ever, so strong it kept threatening to knock us down. The old man was away hunting. Tall clouds, white and billowing, were sailing by in a warm blue sky just like the summer clouds I'd seen in Arizona when my father and I had gone up to see the Grand Canyon.

Fifty-five degrees above zero. Except for a twenty- or thirty-foot strip of ice clinging to both shores, the wide Nahanni was running open water. Suddenly I could think only of escape, and I was already picturing how we could do it.

"It's been two weeks, and we haven't heard any airplanes," I said, breaking our long silence on the subject. When Raymond didn't respond, I said, "Clint told me that people canoe this river in the summer."

Raymond said, "You have a canoe stashed in the bush?"

I was thinking as fast as I could. "No, but maybe we could make a raft!"

Raymond didn't seem too sure about the idea.

"We could make a raft from the logs down below

the falls,'' I told him. "We could tie them together with parachute cord. That stuff's really strong. Maybe we could make it out of here before the river freezes again!''

"You're thinking the river must be easy because they can do it in canoes,'' Raymond said. "This is a dangerous river. I know a guy who guides people down the river in the summer—they use spray covers over the tops of the canoes, to keep them from getting swamped. There's bad rapids in those canyons. What do we know about that? How could we get through?''

"I rafted the Rio Grande twice with my dad, out in west Texas. That had some big rapids, and we got through okay. We didn't have a guide either—it was just us. Don't we have to try?''

Raymond seemed to be coming around a little. I saw a flicker of hope in his eyes, the hope that we could escape down this river while we still had a chance.

"What choice do we have?'' I asked him. Suddenly I found myself losing control, letting all my fears rise to the surface. "We're running out of food fast. *Help is not on the way*, Raymond. What do we have, a couple boxes of fruit, some beans, two macaroni-and-cheese dinners? We're starving as it is. Do you really think we can survive the winter out here?''

"No,'' Raymond agreed. "I can't picture it.''

"When will this river break up in the spring, if we don't go for it now?''

"Early May.''

"You're kidding.''

I could see he wasn't. "Well?'' I asked him.

10

We wasted no more time talking; we never even agreed to it in words. We looked at each other, then scooped up the things we needed—the ax and the bow saw, the parachute cord—and ran through the forest, then down the portage trail around the falls.

We went straight to the giant driftpile on the beach. The falls had stripped off every branch and even peeled the bark from the logs. We selected logs seven or eight inches in diameter, cut them free, and hauled them downstream to a sandy spot on the shore that was mostly out of range of the drenching mist from the falls.

Some of the logs that looked good turned out to be completely waterlogged. Over the thundering of the falls, Raymond said to forget about them. We had to keep the raft as light as possible if it was going to be maneuverable at all.

Using the ax, we notched two of the logs near the ends, then laid two others across them at right angles and lashed the joints with parachute cord. Then we started laying logs across the top of our rectangular frame and lashing them down. It was going to be a crude raft, that was for sure—about sixteen feet long and twelve feet across. We had half the deck logs in place before we slowed down enough to start thinking about how we were going to steer it.

"Johnny could help us make oars," Raymond said. "He makes canoe paddles for people all the time. It's got to be birch, I know that—there's birch near our camp. He could pick the right ones. They're going to have to be pretty long."

"And we'll have to row standing up. Side by side, one of us on each oar, don't you think? And what about oarlocks?"

Oarlocks took some figuring. Raymond got the idea of making them from stout, Y-shaped branches in the shape of giant slingshots. The oar would rest on the fork of the Y, and the fork would stand a couple of feet above the surface of the raft.

Raymond looked around quickly, then pointed to a thicket of bushy trees he said were alders, over by the switchbacks at the bottom of the trail. We ran over there, found the forked branches he'd envisioned, and cut out our oarlocks with the bow saw. All the time we were racing, knowing the Chinook couldn't last.

By the time darkness was falling—around three-thirty—we were nearly done with the raft itself. We had a little more work to do on the oarlocks, but we could do that first thing tomorrow, maybe while Johnny worked on the oars. We'd been working in such a frenzy we hadn't even thought about being hungry. We started up the steep trail that led to the top of the falls.

The old man wasn't in camp. "Maybe he got a moose," Raymond said.

"Either that or something's happened to him," I said. I grabbed the flashlight, which by now wasn't worth much, and we started upriver. About a mile from camp we saw a dark shape coming our way. The old man's parka hood was thrown back; we could make out the patch of snow-white hair.

"You get a moose?" Raymond asked him.

Johnny Raven broke into a smile. "Moose," Johnny repeated, bringing his hands close together as if to say "small moose." First I thought he was saying he'd shot a small moose, maybe a calf, but then he started leading us back toward camp.

"Maybe he only saw one," Raymond said, disappointed. I began to wonder how we were going to explain to Johnny about the raft.

Once back in camp, the old man collected the skinning knife and the whetstone, the frying pan, a couple of cooking pots, and the red wool blanket. Raymond and I looked at each other, wondering what was going on. Johnny threw some rose hips into one of the pots and arranged the other things in the packsack. Then he motioned for us to follow him.

"He really got one!" Raymond exclaimed, beaming. "He got a moose, and he's taking us to go eat at the moose."

Sky-high with expectation, we followed the old man upstream to the carcass of an enormous bull moose. I just stood there, astonished at the reality of it lying dead right in front of us. Johnny had already gutted it. Here was a mountain of meat—the antlers measured at least five feet across. I let out a victory whoop and asked Raymond, "How much would this moose weigh?"

"Over a thousand pounds for sure," he replied, "maybe a lot more."

"How come he said it was a little one?"

Raymond laughed. "That's just like those old guys. They never brag—it's bad luck."

I was already wondering how we were going to get all this meat down to the raft. We couldn't afford the time. The arctic air could come back and freeze the river real quick.

The old man was skinning the moose by the flickering beam of Raymond's flashlight. I got a fire going with the butane lighter and some shredded birchbark from my daypack, like the old man always used. By this time I'd caught on to always having some handy. The birchbark caught quickly and flamed hot, giving off black smoke from all the resin in it. Johnny Raven brought over a big hunk of fat, which I started melting in the pan, and then he returned shortly with the tongue of the moose, indicating I should cook it in the pan. It wouldn't have been my first choice.

Raymond cut thick filets for us from the tenderloin along the backbone. We skewered them with sticks and roasted them suspended above the fire. The moment a piece began to look about halfway cooked, I removed it from the fire and sliced it into thin strips with my pocket knife for Raymond and me. Johnny, we could see, was waiting for the tongue, which was sizzling and spattering in the pan.

I started wolfing down huge mouthfuls of meat. Johnny reached over and touched my arm, cautioning me to slow down. I followed his advice, chewing more slowly, but the meat was so delicious and I was so hungry I kept eating until my stomach felt like a cement mixer. Then I drank some tea. "Should we tell him about the raft now?" I asked Raymond.

"I think wait until tomorrow morning," he said. "I

kind of hate to make him think about anything else. Just let him enjoy his moose."

Raymond and I returned to the brush teepee. Johnny spent the night upriver by the moose, sitting by the fire and keeping guard. "Against wolves or bears," Raymond said. "People say bears can smell something dead from miles away."

The warm Chinook kept blowing: forty degrees above zero, even into the night. So far our luck was holding.

A couple of hours before first light we built up the signal fire and headed back to the old man. We wanted to eat some more of the moose and then get the oars made as soon as possible. As soon as we'd eaten our fill, Raymond began to explain to the old man what we had decided to do. At first Raymond tried in English, speaking slowly and simply, but he had to give that up. Then he quickly gathered up some little sticks, snapped them into lengths, and made a model of the raft. I kept watching the old man's face as Raymond acted out a rowing motion. Just that quickly, the old man was wagging his head. "No," he said. "No good." He pointed straight down at the ground. "Camp here," he said.

"Try again," I told Raymond. "He doesn't understand that we could get all the way down the river, get out of here."

Raymond tried again. But old Johnny Raven understood perfectly well. He started talking rapidly in his own language, shaking his head all the while. He went to the bank of the Nahanni and came back with a big chunk of ice in his hands. He set it down squarely in front of Raymond's model raft.

"What's that supposed to mean?" I asked.

"I guess that we'll get stopped by ice," Raymond

said. "I guess he's saying that the river will freeze up again before we get out."

"Well, what does *he* think we should do?" I asked, all out of patience.

"I think he wants us to move camp here, to the moose. That's what they used to do in the old days. In the winter they would move to the moose someone had killed. They'd stay there until they'd eaten the whole moose, and tanned the hide and so on. We'd have to build another brush teepee here."

The old man stood up and spread his arms wide, then imitated the sound of a droning airplane motor. Apparently he still thought we were going to be rescued.

"What if it doesn't come?" I shouted.

"I know, I know," Raymond said. "Even so, he thinks we should stay here. I guess he's thinking we could make dry meat from most of the moose, to preserve it, and just wait for the airplane."

"Along about January that would get old," I said.

The old man's eyes, which usually were looking away, were now going from Raymond's to mine and back. He was wild with frustration, not being able to talk to us. He reached for the rifle and emptied the magazine of shells—three of them. Then he held up three fingers.

"What's that supposed to mean?" I said. "Showing us he killed the moose with one shot? I thought they never bragged."

Raymond said, "He wants to make sure we know he still has three left. I guess he's thinking—hoping—we can get a lot more meat."

The old man was pointing upstream. "Moose . . . sheep . . . caribou," he said in English. Then he pointed downstream, and he made a cutting motion with his fingers, right across his throat.

Raymond said, "Looks to me like he's saying that down in the canyons there won't be any game. Upstream we can get more meat."

"So what's more important?" I asked hotly. "Being where there's more game or getting out of here?"

"I don't know," Raymond said slowly. "I guess that's the question."

"How long would this moose last us?"

"I don't know exactly. Maybe a couple of months."

"And the river breaks up in early May. What are we talking about now, *spending the winter?*"

"I guess that's why he showed us the shells. Johnny must think it could be done."

From the corner of my eye I spotted some motion. It was a raven flying from the top of a tree to the ground by the moose. The huge black bird was looking at us carefully with its slanted black eyes, then looking back at the moose. It took a few hops closer, looked at us again.

The old man paid little attention to the scruffy-looking raven.

I said to Raymond, "You said you have to be lucky to get a moose. What if his luck runs out!"

"It would be just like back in the old days," Raymond said. "Sometimes people starved. He knows that. He was there."

I started counting on my fingers. "November—December—January—February—March—April—May."

I could see the uncertainty in Raymond's face. He wasn't sure I was right. He was actually considering spending the winter here. "You've got to be kidding!"

80

I said, and I could feel my face flush. "You just admitted we could starve to death!"

"These old guys know a lot," he said defensively. "We should at least listen to what he's saying."

"You can't even speak his language!"

Raymond turned away, like I'd hit him with a whip.

"Look," I said, trying to calm down. "Take a look at the river, will you? It's running open!"

His eyes were digging a hole in the ground. "I know," he said.

I noticed the raven tearing at a scrap of flesh sticking out from the hide. I picked up a hefty stick and heaved it at the raven as hard as I could. I almost hit it. The raven protested with a loud squawk as it rose with heavy wingbeats, landing back in the top of the spruce.

The old man was distressed, biting his lip, looking from me over to Raymond.

"Don't ever do that!" Raymond snapped, looking at me as if I was a stranger and an idiot. "Scare him off, but don't hurt him," Raymond said.

"You scare him off next time," I snapped back.

I was all worked up. I reached for the ax. "I'm going to make the oars myself and finish the raft," I told him. "If the river's still open when I finish, I'm going to go. I'll take a little of the moose meat and I'll take one of the waterproof boxes, for my sleeping bag. I'll just take a few things—you guys can keep everything else. *Spend the winter back here?* I don't think so. I'd rather take my chances on the river. I want you to come with me, Raymond, but if you decide to stay, no hard feelings."

Raymond walked away, sat down on a log. I stood there waiting. I knew I wanted him with me. I'd need him to help manage the raft.

The old man was cutting scraps from the carcass and flicking them over toward the spruce. The raven swooped to the ground and started hopping around, picking up the scraps and swallowing them whole as the old man spoke to the shaggy-throated bird in his language.

At last Raymond stood up. He went to his great-uncle, not to me. He said, "I'm sorry, Johnny. I'm not like you. You used to live out on the land. Maybe you still can. Maybe you just think you can do it, even though you only have three bullets. You aren't so young anymore, Johnny. Maybe you just want to live the way you used to one more time. I know how you elders think it was much better back then—that's what you're always saying. But this is now, don't you see?"

The old man may not have understood the words, but it was apparent from the mournful expression on his gentle face that he understood completely that Raymond had sided with me. He looked older than ever, immeasurably sad. "Okay," he said softly. "Okay, Raymond."

To my surprise the old man got up, came over to me, and made a short speech to me in his own language. I was struck by his frailty, yet awed by his great dignity. For a moment I was ashamed that I had won Raymond away from him. He put his hand out. I started to shake it, then realized he was asking for the ax that was in my hand.

"He's going to help us make the oars," Raymond explained. "He's going to come with us."

11

I t had been all we could do to get the old man to leave that moose behind and get on the raft. Old Johnny must have been thinking we'd wait until the following day; he'd only roughed out the semblance of oars. But the Chinook winds seemed to be letting up and we were in a panic to get going.

We had a couple of hundred pounds of meat on the raft and even the moose hide, which Johnny had insisted upon, but we'd broken the old man's heart leaving so much of the animal behind. Raymond felt awful about it. "Johnny'll never have any luck with moose again," he muttered on our last portage around the falls. That's when Raymond walked to the edge of the cliffs at Virginia Falls, right out over the brink, and heaved his electric guitar into the maelstrom. Raymond's mouth was like a jagged scar on his face.

By the time we finally pushed off and started down through choppy water into the painted canyon, the stony slopes of Sunblood Mountain were glowing blood-red in the late sun. It was the sixteenth of November. Each of us was wearing a pair of Raymond's gym shoes, having crammed our winter boots and Johnny's tall moccasins into our limited dry storage along with changes of clothing, our sleeping bags, and Johnny's blanket.

The river narrowed between cliffs that were splashed with reds and yellows, and the raft was funneled into a train of high waves. Standing at the oars, struggling to try to get control of the raft, Raymond and I were barely managing to stay on our feet. It looked like our oarlocks were going to work well enough, but we'd have to figure out better what we were trying to do with the oars if we were going to actually control the raft, as heavy as it was.

Every time the raft wallowed through a wave, the entire deck was awash with water. At the back, the old man was sitting atop the bigger piece of moose meat, the better part of a hindquarter, hanging on to the cord that tied the meat down. The army boxes and the rest of the gear was lashed down toward the front. My feet hurt so much with the cold I wanted to scream. The water temperature couldn't have been but a few degrees above freezing. I had to tell myself that our feet would be okay despite the pain, as long as the air temperature stayed above freezing too.

As we rounded a bend I glanced back and saw the falls vanish. Bigger than life one moment, the central fact of our lives, gone the next. Another bend in the river and Raymond gave a shout. He was pointing toward a driftpile of jumbled logs at the tip of an island in the middle of the river. Then I saw he was pointing at a piece of metal just above the waterline. A piece of the Cessna, I thought.

"Let's get to shore!" I yelled, and we spun the raft sideways in the current, rowing as hard as we could for shore. The island was slipping by despite our efforts. It looked as if we weren't going to make it, but finally we were able to reach calmer water, and we beached at the bottom tip of the island.

My feet hurt with each step as we hobbled back up to the big driftpile. I was afraid of what we might find there, but I knew we had to look. I walked out onto a log that was sawing up and down with the current. It was a piece of wing that was showing. A length of cable stuck out of both ends and trailed in the water. There was nothing else to be seen.

I turned to go, but now the old man walked out onto the log, and he squatted down and began to yank on the cable, trying to free it. "We're losing daylight," I fretted.

The old man persisted. I didn't want to yell at him.

All three of us pulled on the cable together, and it tore free, about fifteen feet of it. "I suppose it will come in handy," I said. "It's a lot stronger than parachute chord. Let's get going!"

Once we got back into the current, the rapids never let up. We lurched and spun, sloshed and wallowed through miles of canyon lined with slabs of rock fallen from the cliffs and pinnacles above. We struck a few rocks that decided to let us by and barely avoided several boulders that would have thrown us all into the river had we breached on them. We rounded a bend and Raymond yelled, "Sweeper!" Barely, just barely, we managed to avoid a tall spruce tree that had fallen into the river yet remained rooted to the bank. By now the day was going dim and we had nowhere to land. I began to wonder if we were going to be trapped out on the river by the darkness.

It was all but dark when the canyon walls gave way on the right, where a creek was splashing into the river through a gravel bar. We were exhausted by the time we worked the raft to the shallows, but pleased at how well we were working together now. We had so much more control of the raft than before.

Fortunately, the beach was littered with driftwood. We built up a fire. It felt good to get into some dry clothes, especially dry boots. We erected a framework of poles all around the fire to begin the slow process of drying our wet clothes without burning them. "How far do you think we came today?" I asked Raymond. "It felt like a lot of miles to me," I added hopefully.

"Pretty far," Raymond said.

I pressed him. "What I mean is, if it's about two hundred miles from the falls to Nahanni Butte, how many do we have behind us?"

"Your guess is as good as mine. Maybe ten klicks— six miles or so?"

All at once the wind turned around and started blowing from a different direction. I was worried enough to dig out the compass. Clint had said the Chinook blows from the west. This wind was blowing from the northeast. The old man saw me looking at the compass. He knew exactly what I was thinking. I felt sick, knowing what this meant. There was no doubting that this was air coming down from the Arctic Ocean, not the Pacific. Johnny Raven knew his directions without a compass, and he'd already figured out that the Chinook was over.

Johnny offered me some rose hip tea. It tasted warm and good, but it did nothing to calm my fears.

The old man spoke at great length around the campfire that night, telling a long story to Raymond, who

86

couldn't understand him. Even so, Raymond was listening, listening intently as if he understood every word. I think it helped him somehow to calm himself down.

Remembering how fast the river could freeze up, I was too nervous to sleep. I could still feel the rumbling of the falls through the ground. I kept seeing the plane crashing against the rock, Clint being thrown into the whitewater. I kept wondering if my father was still searching. I thought he would be. But how could he find us down here?

By morning my worst fears were realized. The river was running cakes of hissing, colliding ice. The Nahanni had dropped several feet as water had formed ice, leaving the raft stranded a hundred feet away from the water across a beach of gravel and ice. Raymond came up from behind me. I could see it in his face, the enormity of our mistake. I said, "Is there any way we can go back to where we were? Do you think there's a trail upstream? Maybe we could hike back?"

I felt sick to my stomach, waiting for him to speak. He chewed on his lip, shook his head. "There's no trail. Like you saw, the canyon is straight up and down. I remember that canoe guide telling me that the only place there's a trail along the river is the portage around the falls."

"I feel so bad," I said. "I talked you into this."

Raymond shrugged. "Too late now," he said. "We better get the raft unstuck and get it back to the water. It's a race with the ice now. The sooner we get going, the better our chances."

We could only manage to drag the raft a few feet at a time. The old man wanted to help us, but Raymond wouldn't let him. It took an agony of effort and precious time before we were able to drag it all the way to the river.

We started downriver again, this time wearing our winter boots. Even if they were going to get wet, we knew we needed some insulation on our feet now. We just had to hope that the air temperature didn't get low enough for frostbite.

Around the bend we encountered a break in the canyons where steep forested mountainsides met the river. There was hardly any current for miles, no whitewater at all but plenty of sweepers. Our feet were staying warm and dry. We pushed hard on the oars to try to gain any speed compared to simply floating. The river split and meandered among islands below the mountains that rose and rose until they vanished in swirling clouds.

We kept pushing along with the hissing ice as the day froze into a changeless gray. As we rounded a bend we heard whitewater. The old man gave a quick cry, and then I saw the river up ahead rushing in a line of waves straight up against a rock wall fifty feet high where the river was making a sharp left-hand turn. To the right, there was an enormous whirlpool where the water that hadn't made the turn was swirling in a vicious circle. All the current in the river was rampaging straight toward the wall. "We gotta pull left!" I yelled to Raymond. Our only chance to avoid crashing into the wall was to try to break out of the current and cross into a lesser whirlpool on the left side.

We rowed with all we had. But the current was too strong and the raft too cumbersome, and we were being swept right down the current line toward the wall.

As we neared the wall I saw that the force of the river had undercut it, and we were going to be pushed under that overhang. In an instant, all three of us threw ourselves on the raft, and I heard an oar shatter. It was mine—I saw the sharp broken shaft pass right by my head. Now the raft was spun around and wedged in against the wall, pinned, with the river streaming up against us. I knew the raft couldn't stay together long under this much pressure. Raymond and I scrambled across the raft and tried to push off the cliff with our legs. I caught a glimpse of the old man scrambling for something to hang on to.

I don't know what it was that freed us, but now we were bumping down the cliff under that low overhang. The raft was spinning; suddenly we both realized that the old man was missing.

"Johnny!" Raymond yelled, and we looked all around, but he was nowhere to be seen. Without a life jacket, I realized, he didn't have a chance.

The raft was bumping alongside the wall again, and still we couldn't see him. The wall ended, and the raft lumbered into the last part of the rapid. Suddenly I spotted the thatch of white hair and Johnny's face bobbing in the waves, barely behind the raft. I gave a yell, and Raymond saw him too. Raymond lunged across the raft and reached, grabbing the old man by the parka hood, as the raft drifted into the slow water below the rapid. We hauled Johnny back onto the raft, where he lay on his side, barely breathing. "He must've been caught under the raft," Raymond said. Johnny's cloth parka was freezing solid as we watched. I thought he was going to die right there before we could get him to shore.

Trying to do what we could with one oar, it must have taken us a mile before we were able to reach some shallows. I jumped out with the braided parachute cord we were using for a bowline and dragged the raft a little closer. Raymond and I were shaking violently from the cold; the old man was beyond shivering and had a glassy look in his eyes. Raymond stripped Johnny's clothing off for him. I was shocked: the old man was nothing but skin and bones.

Raymond spread out the blue tarp and helped Johnny into a sleeping bag while I fumbled with frozen fingers, trying to get a fire started. At last I succeeded, and we ran around in our wet boots collecting driftwood to add to the fire. Finally we could change clothes and start to dry out our boot liners. It took hours for Johnny to come around. We'd been within a thread of losing him.

I said to Raymond, "Johnny was right all along, and you told me we should listen to him. This is all my fault. I'm sorry."

Raymond shrugged. " 'Sorry,' that's famous last words."

"Well, I mean it," I told him.

His dark eyes flashed, and he said, "It was just as much me as it was you. I should've known better. It's because I don't know anything. I don't know hardly any more than you do about winter out on the land. I got scared."

"So what do we do now?"

"Make a new oar, I guess."

Raymond found a birch and started working on the new oar. We had to spend the night there, huddling by the fire. As we put out into the ice-filled river the next day, I said to Raymond that I couldn't get over how Johnny could have survived that swim. Raymond said, "He spent most of his life out in the cold. Those old people are used to it. That nurse in the hospital in Yellowknife . . .'' He laughed.

I was amazed he could laugh about anything, given our circumstances.

''When I came to the hospital to get him, she said he was the hardest guy to give shots to that she ever met in her life—it was really a challenge to get through his skin.''

''No kidding?''

''She said she had to ram that needle, at just the right angle. . . .'' Raymond pointed at his own backside, and laughed. ''She said his skin was tougher than moose hide. 'From being out in the cold so much of his life,' she explained. She was Dene herself—she knew.''

That night we camped at the mouth of a creek that joined the Nahanni from the right side. We spent the night huddling close to the fire, dozing off a little, but we had to keep the fire going, and every so often we had to go down and push the raft into open water. The shallow water was icing up fast, and we knew the raft could get locked in solid if we didn't watch it.

The next day we entered a much deeper canyon. This one towered thousands of feet above us, pitted with caves and broken every mile or two with forested draws that came all the way down to the river. At one point the river narrowed and passed between a sheer wall on the right, which rose a thousand feet or more, and a massive stranded pinnacle on the left that had trees growing from its top.

All the time, our channel of free water in the middle of the river was shrinking as the ice cakes coming down the river adhered to the ice growing along the shores. We pushed on, rowing as hard as we could down the narrowing passage. The river swung slowly through the canyons, bend after bend. Unlike us, it had all the time in the world.

The next day the canyon seemed to die out at first, but within a few miles we were back under towering walls, and the canyon seemed even more constricted than before. In some places the riverbed was only a couple of hundred feet wide from wall to wall. We steered our way around immense boulders with logs perched on top, left there by floods, I guessed.

The freezing clouds dropped down inside the canyon and clung to the walls and the pinnacles. We were floating now among great blocks of ice that jostled us for position, and we fended them off with driftwood poles we'd picked up along the shore. We were stunned to hear a motor suddenly, the unmistakable drone of an airplane. "Where is it?" I asked desperately, hoping it would appear for a second in the clouds.

"Heading upstream," Raymond said, pointing where Johnny was pointing. "And it's flying high . . . it's just about gone . . . they're going someplace else, someplace where it's safe to fly under the clouds. They can't fly down in the canyon with these clouds, that's for sure."

I knew what he was thinking. "Up above the falls," I said. "That's where they're going to look." Suddenly I pictured my father inside that airplane. If we had only stayed put . . . Could our signal fire still be burning, still barely smoking? I knew that was impossible. We hadn't even built it up on the day we took off, we were in such a hurry.

I looked at Raymond. He was thinking all the same things I was. He said, "At least now we know they're still searching."

But will they ever think of looking down in the canyons, on the river itself? I wondered. How could they ever guess what we'd done?

Around a bend, I looked downstream and gasped. The ice had formed a dam across the entire width of the river. "Look at that!" I yelled to Raymond.

We were suddenly stopped dead in a rising lake full of ice floes. I thought this was the end. Raymond and the old man obviously thought so too. We quit rowing; there was nothing to be done. There was no shore to go to, no way to get around the dam, just sheer canyon walls on both sides. Johnny stood up for a better look, studied the ice dam for a long time, then sat back down on the moose meat. We both looked to him for some kind of idea, but his face was blank.

Raymond and I talked a little, but then we just sat down on the duffel bags and waited. I could picture what was going to happen now: the river was going to freeze us in solid right here, maybe sometime during the night.

Out of the silence came a sudden shearing crash, loud as thunder. I wondered for a half second what it was, then jumped up and saw that the ice dam had burst. The lake was pouring through a small gap in the center of the dam. Raymond and I both grabbed the oars. "When it starts to take us,' he said, "really hang on!"

It was no more than a couple of minutes before the raft went surging downstream among the tumbling ice floes. From the corner of my eye I saw Johnny getting down low, bracing his back against the moose quarter. I concentrated on the gap that had broken open in the ice dam, no more than a hundred yards ahead. The gap itself couldn't have been more than thirty feet wide, and the river was pouring through it, down onto a steep chute of whitewater below. We had no choice but to push on the oars, line up dead center for the gap in the dam, and take whatever happened below. "Hang on!" I heard Raymond yell just before we passed through the gap and started down the chute.

Down we plunged, fast, into the very bottom of a deep trough, then rode up, up on the colossal wave cresting below. The raft was slowing as it climbed the wave; I thought we didn't have enough momentum to make it over the very top. We were stalling out, and I realized we were just about to slide back down into the trough.

Raymond could feel it as well. At the same moment, we both pushed on the oars as hard as we could, topped out on the wave, and started down into a series of lesser waves leading to calm water.

I looked around. All three of us were still on the raft. "We did it!" I shouted.

Raymond raised his fist triumphantly. "I can't believe we made it over the top of that thing!"

Johnny was beaming too. I thought, I bet he's never done anything like *that* in his whole long life.

I couldn't help but let my hopes rise. We were moving again, and as far downstream as I could see, it was all calm water. We threaded our way among countless ice floes, many standing up like icebergs.

Midafternoon the canyon opened up onto a wide, forested valley, with a stream coming in from the right that drained mountains standing back at a distance. The left side of the valley was made up of an immense gravel bar below three side canyons that had gouged their way down through a flat escarpment tilting toward the high mountains. A creek ran across the gravel bar toward the Nahanni, entering the river at a dozen places along the shore. I could see the channels picking new paths around ones that had previously frozen shut.

"Deadmen Valley," the old man said, in English. It was apparent that this was a name and a place he knew.

Some miles ahead we could see the narrow gate where Deadmen Valley ended and the Nahanni entered another, deeper canyon. We knew we had no choice but to stay with the river, enter that next canyon, and hope to squeak on through to Nahanni Butte. But as we were nearing the gate of the canyon, we came around a bend and saw that the ice had sealed the surface of the river solid from one bank to the other and as far downriver as we could see. The river was running under the ice from here on. "This is it!" I yelled.

"Get your knife ready to cut stuff loose!" Raymond yelled back.

In another minute we were swept against the ice. We cut all the tie-downs as fast as we could and started unloading the raft. Ice floes were jamming up against the raft, and water was sweeping across us and freezing. "Which shore do we go to?" I shouted. Johnny Raven was pointing to the right side.

We were throwing everything off onto the ice as fast as we could. As I stepped off the raft with the bigger piece of moose meat on my back, I slipped and fell hard on the edge of the ice, landing on my left side without the chance to break my fall. I watched the meat plunge into the river and disappear under the ice. I looked up and saw Raymond's eyes, and the old man's, staring where the meat had disappeared. Suddenly I realized how bad my left side hurt, where I'd cracked a rib in football.

I stumbled around in a delirium, shuttling gear up to the top of the riverbank and helping Raymond with the heavy frozen moose hide. After that I went back to the raft but found we'd already taken everything off it. I recovered the bowline we'd braided from parachute cord, then watched as the raft buckled and went under the ice. Then I trudged up the bank and fell in a heap, stricken with remorse that hurt much worse than the pain in my side.

Raymond was starting a fire with birchbark and kitchen matches. "It only makes sense we'd have bad luck with moose," I heard him mutter. "Leaving all that meat behind."

The old man stood on the top of the bank, taking the measure of Deadmen Valley, watching the cold wind bend the trees down. He was scanning the high mountains that had us encircled. What was he thinking? Were we going to stay here now? Our remaining moose meat couldn't have weighed twenty-five pounds. But Johnny had those three bullets. Our lives were in his hands now.

A quick fire and dry clothes, a lean-to and a night's supply of firewood, then darkness. A little dried fruit to eat and the howling of wolves across the river. I was utterly exhausted, and I had a deep ache in my side, pain whenever I breathed or moved. Had I recracked the rib? "Wolves in the valley should mean moose," Raymond grunted in my direction.

Johnny Raven was looking into the fire as he warmed his hands and feet. He seemed to be letting his mind drift, and I couldn't blame him. How did he keep going? For such a gentle man he was tough as nails.

"This bare ground will make tough moose hunting," Raymond said, holding out his hands to the fire and stamping his feet. "I wish it would snow about four or five feet—that's when the moose stick to just a few trails so they can get around. Sometimes they stand right in our snowmobile trails—won't even get out of the way.''

"I can't believe we're hoping for snow, but I see what you mean. Could we even get around?''

"We've got the moose hide. Johnny can make snowshoes now. Tomorrow, I bet he finds some birch and starts making the frames.''

"Without him . . .'' I didn't want to finish my thought.

Raymond finished it for me: "Without him we're dead meat.''

The old man stood up. By the light of the fire, he started stowing what was left of our moose meat in one of the army boxes. Then he picked up the rifle, motioned for us to follow him, and started to walk away. I was confused, and so was Raymond. Where did he want us to go? I wasn't about to force an explanation from him, that was for sure. I thought of grabbing the flashlight, then remembered it was dead. As the crescent moon disappeared behind the mountains towering over the valley we walked into the darkness, following his silhouette.

Beyond the firelight the stars were blazing in the brittle, dry air. Even with only a few patches of crusted snow here and there to reflect the starlight, my eyes adjusted and I could make out where I was going. We followed the old man upriver as, from nowhere and everywhere, curtains of iridescent green and yellow light materialized in the night sky, swirling and shimmering and dancing. The northern lights. My father had often told me about them, the aurora borealis. I stopped to stare at the dazzling aurora shifting in a moment from horizon to horizon, returning just as fast, this time like brilliant searchlights. I ran to catch up, and then I walked with my eyes on the eerie lights and their strange, shifting shapes.

Where a small creek, almost frozen shut, reached the Nahanni, the old man turned away from the river and led us into the big trees. Then he pointed, and we could make out a small cabin in a clearing up ahead. The cabin was glowing yellow-green under the light of the aurora, and it looked like an apparition. Nearby stood a food cache on tall stilts. "Patterson," the old man said, pointing at the cabin.

"Johnny knew about this place!" Raymond exclaimed. "He must have been here before."

Johnny Raven fashioned a torch from a rolled piece of birchbark. By its light we lifted the cabin's latch and swung the door open on creaking hinges. We stepped over the doorsill, which was the shaved top of the second log up from the ground. The torchlight fell on a small woodstove in the corner and sections of stovepipe lying on the dirt floor. About thirteen feet square and tall enough for us to stand even in the corners, the cabin had a couple of shelves and a crude handmade table— that was all there was to it. Above the table, the initials *RMP* and *GM* were carved large on the logs, along with the inscription *Deadmen Valley 1927*. The old man pointed at the initials and repeated that name, "Patterson."

"A trapper?" Raymond muttered to his great-uncle, and the old man nodded his agreement.

"You knew him?" Raymond asked. He pointed at

the name, and then looked back to the old man. "You knew him?"

Johnny was nodding vigorously.

We returned to our campfire for the night. Raymond and I stayed up close to the fire as Johnny wrapped himself in his blanket, lay down, and slept. "At least we have a cabin to stay in now," I said. "A cabin with a stove—we can stay warm. Do you think that plane will come back, take a look around here?"

"We should get a signal fire going in case it does," Raymond said. "Maybe build it here and use driftwood, so we can save the wood near the cabin for the stove."

"I just wish I hadn't lost that meat. You're pretty lucky to have me along, you know. You wouldn't want this to be too easy."

With a grin, Raymond said, "If I ever do another raft trip, I think I'd want to have you with me. You're pretty good on those oars." He placed a big chunk of wood on the fire. "Johnny'll get another moose," he said confidently.

"Do you think Johnny wants us to stay here for the rest of the winter—if no one spots us, I mean?"

"Maybe we'll be able to hike out down the river later, on the ice, once there's no more Chinooks. I just don't know. I think we better just take our cues from Johnny from here on out."

"You won't get any back talk from me on that."

In the gray morning twilight we built up our signal fire by the river, then began moving our stuff. The squat cabin with its thick roof of moss and clay looked as miraculous as before. We broomed the dirt floor clean with spruce branches, brought our gear inside, and moved in. The stove looked to be in one piece. We fitted the stovepipe back together and ran it up through the roof jack. The big roof poles looked sound. The one window had been broken out, but a sheet of hard clear plastic had been fastened across the entire window frame. The window allowed quite a bit of light. "Home," Raymond announced. It was the twenty-first of November.

We tried a fire in the rusty little stove. It worked, and cheered us up as we warmed our hands.

I looked around the cabin, ending up with my eyes on the rough little table. "This must be the kitchen," I said.

"Needs a microwave," Raymond added. "No TV in here either. Next time we should bring a VCR—watch movies all winter."

"There you go," I said, with a small laugh that made my side hurt. But in the back of my mind, I was remembering Clint's story about the two brothers who tried to winter in Deadmen Valley, starved to death, and lost their heads to the bears.

The old man pegged the moose hide to the wall with the old nails we found around the place and began scraping the hair from the hide with the sheath knife. He was going to make it into rawhide—babiche, as Raymond called it. Raymond and I sawed three big rounds of spruce to serve as stools. We allowed our spirits to lift for the time being. All that remained of our food was a little flour, baking powder, some beans, a handful of dried fruit, and the box of meat.

Raymond and I fashioned a ladder so we'd be able to reach the food cache behind the cabin, trusting that meat would come to fill it. Like a cabin in miniature on stilts, the old cache was supported by four trees that had been sawed off about twelve feet above the ground. Just under the cache, the stilts were wrapped with stove-pipe—to prevent a black bear or wolverine from reaching the cache, Raymond said.

"What about a grizzly?" I asked.

"Grizzlies can't climb," he explained. "And it's out of a grizzly's reach."

As Raymond had predicted, the old man took us out right away on a hunt for just the right birch tree. He had us cut a ten-foot log from it and carry it back to the cabin, where he planed it flat on two sides with the ax and began to strip it into lengths. "The old guys like Johnny always use birch for snowshoe frames," Raymond said. "It's tough, it'll bend without breaking, and it splits easily when it's cold."

Around noon the next day it cleared up enough for us to notice the sun making a brief appearance over the bald mountain to the southwest. The temperature was ten below, practically a heat wave. When I returned from building up the signal fire, I found Raymond watching intently as Johnny fashioned a snowshoe frame, bending the green birch strips patiently over his knee, bracing and lashing them temporarily into shape with whittled pegs and fine spruce roots. I watched for a while, until Johnny picked up his rifle, said something to us in Slavey, and slipped into the trees. He returned in the dark—no luck.

On the twenty-fifth of November the warm Chinook returned. By day it would blow through the valley almost at gale force, and by night we could hear it high above, raging on the ridges. The Nahanni opened up in spots, smoking in the cold mornings. The Chinook would alternate with the arctic winds in pitched battles that seesawed back and forth above Deadmen Valley, sending the temperature from forty above to thirty below.

Still no snow. It was not the weather that Raymond had hoped for as Johnny hunted our side of the river for the moose that should be browsing in the willow thickets. Raymond and I were picking frozen cranberries. Any we could find helped a little. We'd gone through the last of the fruit and the flour, and the ration of meat we were allowing ourselves could barely keep us going. We still had beans. For our only meal of the day, we'd been allowing ourselves no more than one pound total of the moose meat, cooked in with some beans.

When the old man wasn't hunting, he was weaving the intricate babiche lacing to complete the first pair of snowshoes. Raymond and I were making snares, braiding the thin strips of babiche as Johnny had shown us. We set a dozen snares up and down the river for snowshoe hares. Raymond knew exactly how to do it, having snared the rabbits with picture wire when he was a kid. He'd bend a young tree down over a rabbit run and rig the snare below it so it made a circle about four inches across, about three inches above the trail. Then he'd arrange slender sticks like a fence on both sides of the snare and tiny ones underneath, so the rabbit was forced to pass through the circle.

Once we interrupted a chase in the trees above us. A dark-furred animal the size of an overgrown house cat hunched its back and growled at us as we passed below. "Marten," Raymond said. In the next tree a red squirrel chattered as the marten glowered at us, growling all the while, trying at the same time to keep its eye on the squirrel. I tried to knock the marten from the tree with a stick but succeeded only in chasing it away.

Raymond was always on the lookout for fresh moose sign, but he wasn't finding any. "All these willow thickets," he kept saying. "All these moose paths. Old droppings everywhere, but none fresh. I don't understand it."

The old man showed Raymond that the airplane cable we have salvaged could make a snare too, just like a rabbit snare, only on a bigger scale. "It's illegal," Raymond said. "But in Deadmen Valley," he added with a smile, "we might get away with it." We rigged the snare on one of the more prominent moose paths through the thickets. As Raymond secured the free end to a cottonwood tree, he said, "Man, would I like to get a moose for Johnny. That's the way it's supposed to be. The young men are supposed to bring the first and the best meat to the elders."

Wherever we went we took the ax with us, for protection. "Nobody walks around in the bush without a rifle," Raymond said.

I told him, "That looks more like an ax you've got in your hand."

"Better than a kick in the knee."

"Where did you come up with that expression? My mother always used to say that."

"Old Dene saying," he replied with a smirk.

"The ax . . . it's protection from what?"

"Bull moose, cow moose with a calf, or 'keep out of its way.' "

"I thought grizzlies were supposed to be hibernating by now."

"Supposed to be," he replied.

With the ax and the bow saw we made so much firewood for our little stove it looked like we had a woodlot going. We sought out the dead trees and hauled them back in lengths to the cabin and sawed and split firewood endlessly, mixing in green spruce, which split easily in the cold. With the Chinook in retreat, perhaps for good, there was plenty of cold available. We each broke a saw blade sawing too fast. When the second one broke a few days after the first, it scared us. We'd have to baby the bow saw now that we were down to the last blade.

The mercury stayed down around twenty and thirty below at midday. It amazed me that life could go on. Yet as long as we dried our clothes out overnight, and dried our gloves and mitts and the felt liners from our boots, we were okay. Bundled up in as many layers as we were, we'd become accustomed to it.

The old man made a simple hand-held drum from a small piece of moose hide that he stretched over a birch frame. It looked something like a big tambourine. He'd tap out a simple rhythm with a small padded stick, sometimes chanting on into the night. The drum had a hypnotic effect and helped take our minds from our hunger. Just as we never spoke about the search plane that didn't come back, we never talked about our hunger. It clawed at us from the inside, a private torment.

At least it was warm in the cabin. That small a space was easy to heat if we just kept stoking the fire. After we would regretfully snuff out the candle for the evening, we'd lie on the spruce boughs in our bags and watch the bit of firelight from the stove door playing on the drumskin and the ancient face of the drummer. Each evening old Johnny started with a Slavey formula that Raymond knew and translated as "In the Distant Time it is said . . ." Raymond explained that Johnny was telling the stories "of when the world was young."

"What are they about?" I asked.

"Oh, like about Raven, how he made the world and then unmade it so it wasn't perfect anymore, how he made mosquitoes and made water to run downhill, how he'd play tricks on everybody. There's even a story about the flood like the one in the Bible. There's stories about animals back when they were human, stories about giants and supernatural beings, about heroes, about medicine men who could communicate with ravens and even take the shape of ravens . . . The elders have all sorts of stories."

All the time Johnny kept building the snowshoes. My eyes kept going back to the finished pair standing in the corner. They were truly works of art with their graceful curves and intricate rawhide webbing.

On the fifth of December it snowed six inches of dry snow, then cleared off. The sun appeared over the bald mountain only ten minutes before it set again. Raymond and I kept felling trees in the twilight, hauling logs to the cabin, splitting wood, and checking our snares. Over the next week we caught three hares, white as snow and always frozen solid by the time we discovered them. We had to bring the rabbits inside the cabin to warm them up enough to gut and skin them. Some years, Raymond said, the rabbits were everywhere you looked. There was even a legend about hares falling out of the sky like snow.

"Looks like we might have to live on rabbits," I said to Raymond. "The moose meat and beans aren't going to last much longer."

"There's no fat on rabbits," he replied. "We're

going to need to find something with some fat on it. They always say your body needs to burn fat when it gets real cold.''

I could see his face growing thinner, and I knew mine must be, too. I guessed I'd already lost fifteen pounds. The last of our moose meat was soon gone.

I was lucky enough to get a grouse with a well-thrown stick. It was a tasty little morsel, but it didn't take the edge off our hunger. Still no fresh sign of moose, and we hadn't heard wolves since we first arrived. Raymond was worried about not hearing the wolves anymore, and I asked him why. "No wolves means no moose," he said. "The wolves follow the moose in the winter, hoping they can get one in deep snow."

On the morning of the sixteenth of December we opened the cabin door and found Deadmen Valley transformed. Two feet of snow had fallen in the night. All the forest was draped with snow and the high mountains all around had taken on the unreality of a painting. It was all so beautiful and so *clean*, the pure whiteness of it all.

Johnny walked over to the snowshoes in the corner. To my surprise, he was motioning to me. He wanted me to try them out. "Good deal!" I said to Raymond, and we all pulled on some clothes. Outside, Johnny helped me step into them and lace up the bindings, and then I took off like a horse out of the starting gate, I guess. I hadn't gone fifteen feet before I tripped and did a faceplant in the snow. I thrashed around, spitting snow out of my mouth and trying to get back up. But I was getting all entangled, making a spectacle of myself with my arms and legs and those five-foot snowshoes all windmilling around. Raymond and Johnny were laughing their heads off. "Hey, I thought this would be easy!" I called.

As soon as he could quit laughing, Raymond said, "Got to keep your tips up, Gabe, or they get caught in the snow. I think you better let Johnny use those now. It's a good day for him to track moose."

Johnny was still chuckling ten minutes later when he stepped into the snowshoes and laced them on. Raymond handed him the rifle and said, "Good luck, Johnny." Just then we heard wings thrashing the cold air and looked up to see a raven directly above, calling, *"Ggaagga . . . ggaagga."*

Raymond whispered, "It's saying, 'Animal . . . animal.'" It struck me that Raymond said this as a matter of fact. He went on to whisper that ravens were known to lead hunters to game, knowing that they would get their share from what the hunter couldn't use.

The old hunter was watching as the raven tucked its wing and rolled over in the sky before flying on. Johnny winked at Raymond and nodded with a smile. "My father says it's a good-luck sign when a raven does that," Raymond explained. "It means the hunter will have good luck that day."

An hour later we heard the rifle shot loud and clear, upriver, in the cold dry air. "Moose in the cooking pot," I said, certain as if I'd seen it fall. We waited as the hours passed, and then, when Johnny hadn't returned by two, we had misgivings and started after him, postholing our way through the new snow without snowshoes.

We found where the trail of the man first intersected the trail of the moose, fresh with droppings and urine, and then we followed the trail of the man, which looped away from the moose's trail and then came back to it every quarter mile or so. "Johnny was staying downwind," Raymond explained.

We found the rifle cartridge in the snow showing where the old man had stood when he'd fired the shot. As the twilight deepened, we found the place where the moose had bolted and run. No blood in the snow, not a fleck. "I guess Johnny missed," Raymond said. His words hung in the cold air like death.

A raven in a nearby tree caught our attention as it walked back and forth on a dead branch, squawking and squawking. "His belly's empty," Raymond said. "He was counting on a moose dinner tonight. Gabe, I think I better get back to the cabin. My boots got a little wet."

"So did mine," I told him. "We better get back fast."

Johnny was sitting by the stove in his bare feet. He glanced up at us coming in. We were throwing off our boots and our socks. I massaged my toes with my fingers. "They're okay," I told Raymond, and he said, "Mine too."

We could see in the old man's mournful eyes that he'd never caught up with the moose. He looked at Raymond and said something in Slavey.

"No medicine," Raymond told me.

I wondered if they were talking about some medicine that had been prescribed back in the hospital. "Let's look in the first-aid kit," I said.

"Dene medicine," Raymond explained. "It's like power and good luck. Different people have medicine for all sorts of things. Hunters have good medicine for different animals. Johnny thinks his medicine for moose is all gone. It's because of how he left the moose above the falls. When you don't treat an animal respectfully, its spirit is offended, and then you won't have any more medicine with that animal. That's what happened."

"Do you think that could be true? Do you believe it yourself?"

"I don't know," Raymond said. "I've heard that kind of stuff all my life. It's not very scientific, I know. I guess I don't know what I think about it."

"But at least we know there's still moose in Deadmen Valley. And he has two shells left."

"That could've been the last moose," Raymond said. To me, it sounded like he was just as convinced as the old man that we'd destroyed our luck.

A half-Chinook swept briefly into the valley, raising the temperature above freezing and melting the snowpack down to six inches. Just as quickly the Chinook was gone, and the cold returned. This time the mercury plunged to forty below. The Nahanni had frozen solid except for one spot upstream that stayed open for some reason, forming an icy fog that hugged the valley floor along the river. The sun wasn't clearing the bald mountain at noon, so twilight was all we had now, even in the middle of the day.

For a couple of days Raymond and I tried to fish the open spot in the river, jigging the lures from crude poles. It was my idea—Raymond had said that the Nahanni had a reputation as a poor fishing river, something to do with all the silt in it from glaciers at its headwaters. ''I think there's some little graylings in here,'' Raymond said, but if there were, we couldn't catch them. We never even had a bite.

Working long into the nights, Johnny completed Raymond's snowshoes and mine. They'd be ready when the next big snowfall came. I started wondering if it might be possible for us to hike out down the canyon of the

Nahanni. I talked it over with Raymond, and we decided to ask Johnny what he thought. Johnny didn't even have to think about it. He pointed upriver to that smoking patch of open water, and then pointed downstream emphatically. "More," he said in English.

Raymond said, "Johnny means it won't be all frozen solid down there like we think it will be."

"But this patch will freeze over later, right? After a few more weeks of cold? There shouldn't be any open spots anywhere, after a while. We can walk out then. Didn't you say people drive cars over the Liard River on your winter road?"

"That's the Liard—it's slow and wide, and it's out in the open country. I've always heard people say the Nahanni is a tricky river, even in the winter. Maybe that's what they're talking about, that it won't freeze solid, just like Johnny's saying."

We spent the days following the old hunter around Deadmen Valley, setting snares and hauling logs around to help make deadfall traps. We were always keeping an eye out for the few cranberries, currants, blueberries, and raspberries that remained. Rose hips were easier to find, and we were able to keep making tea.

Every time we had to use our bare fingers, we paid the price. Once cold, they took a long time to warm again. At least I had my oversize mittens to pull over my ski gloves. Raymond's wool mittens weren't large enough to accommodate his gloves inside. Johnny had only a pair of winter gloves.

One day Johnny stopped at a certain tree, some sort of pine, and started peeling back the little flakes of bark with the sheath knife. Behind every flake was a blueberry cached for the winter. "Camprobber," the old man said, using their nickname for the gray jays. Raymond started prying out blueberries with his pocket knife, and I joined in, all three of us working on that tree like woodpeckers. It was a tough way to make a meal.

Raymond always wore the packsack, and I had my daypack, in the hope that we might find something to stuff in them and bring home. So far we were collecting just enough small animals from the deadfalls and snares to keep us alive—a few snowshoe hares, a couple of red squirrels, a marten. Along with a few berries and rose hips, that was our diet now. Even in my sleep I was starving.

Sometimes we couldn't find any berries or rose hips. One day the old man made a tea of spruce tips. It tasted awfully pitchy. Raymond said it tasted much better in the spring when the tips were new.

When we went out in the bush with Johnny Raven, we walked quiet as deer. Johnny led with the rifle, Raymond followed, carrying the ax, and I came last. Johnny would never wear the turquoise headband over his ears when he was hunting. I wondered how he could stand the cold and why he hadn't lost his ears to frostbite.

On the twenty-first of December we followed Johnny several miles south, toward the glowing orange horizon. It was my birthday, and it was also the shortest day of the year.

It was Raymond's birthday as well. When I wished him a happy birthday, he was surprised I knew. "It's mine, too," I told him. "We both just turned sixteen. I found out we had the same birthday back at the boarding school, when I was getting my room assignment."

"Who's older, I wonder?" Raymond said as we fol-

113

lowed behind Johnny. "My mother said I was born at eight in the morning."

"I was born at five in the afternoon."

Raymond stopped walking and gave me a poke in the arm. "Happy birthday, little brother."

I had to laugh. It felt good, him calling me that.

Johnny was disappearing ahead of us into the trees. We hustled to catch up and found him inspecting a clearing—a beaver pond, I realized, all frozen over. A huge mound of sticks and mud stuck out of the iron-hard ice, and beaver-chewed aspen stumps circled the pond. "I bet Johnny's wishing he had the stuff he needs for trapping beavers under the ice," Raymond remarked.

"Is that possible?" I wondered aloud.

"My father used to do it back when he had his trapline. You have to be able to figure out where all the beavers' runways out of the main lodge are, where the runways go to the feed pile, and where they have their hideout houses—those are extra places besides the lodge where the beavers can get up and breathe air. You have to be able to read all different kinds of ice and keep a map of everything in your head. They use steel chisels and chain saws to get through the ice down to the runways so they can set the snares."

The old hunter was out on the pond, studying the ice. We watched from the bank, stamped our feet in the cold, and waited while he looked closely at different spots all around the pond and its banks. "What could he be doing?" I asked Raymond.

Johnny marked a spot with a stick, eventually three more. Then he took the ax from Raymond and proceeded to chop away at one of the spots along the bank. At last he exposed a small hollow place with open

114

water. "One of the hideout houses, I think," Raymond said. The old man rested as the water in there froze over in a matter of minutes.

Raymond cut open the second hideout house, and I cut open the third, making the ice chips fly. Raymond said I should slow down. It was dangerous to work up a sweat in this cold and get your clothes wet. The two of us shared the fourth hideout den as Johnny Raven looked on approvingly. Then we began to cut open the main lodge from above. Raymond and I took turns. The sticks and the mud were frozen together like concrete. Finally Raymond broke through into free air. The roof of the lodge had been a little more than a foot thick.

Now we worked to enlarge the hole in the top of the lodge, until we could look in, and then we saw the wide tail of a beaver as the animal splashed into the water from a platform above the waterline. Johnny pulled a long hefty stick free and set it aside. He had us keep working until we had chopped away a good part of the top of the lodge. We could see beavers in the water snatching a breath of air, then disappearing through their runways. After a minute they'd be back. I realized that they were finding their hideout spots frozen shut, then returning to the main lodge, which was the only place where they could breathe.

Johnny Raven began to act out a pantomime for Raymond, throwing in a few English words and a few in Slavey. I thought I knew what he was trying to describe, but it didn't seem possible. I wouldn't have thought Raymond could accept that the old man seemed to be suggesting. But when Raymond turned to me, his dark eyes were filled with determination. He said, "Johnny says the beavers are too big for him to lift. He wants me to get down in there and lift them out. Then you club them with that stick.''

I said, ''Their teeth could take your fingers off!''

Raymond was trying to stay calm. ''He says they'll give their lives to us if we do it right.''

I said, ''Have you ever heard of this before?''

He shook his head. ''Johnny says as long as I don't show any fear I'll be okay. I want to do this. I want to do something for him. He thinks I can do it.''

There was nothing I could say. We needed the meat.

Raymond turned away for a minute to collect his thoughts. Then he took off his gloves and climbed bare-handed into the lodge, kneeling on the beavers' platform, keeping still. I held my breath. After a few minutes the commotion in the water ceased. Five beavers were resting their chins on their platform as if they were waiting for Raymond to take them, just as the old man had said.

I stole a glance at Raymond's eyes, which were focused on the eyes of one of the animals. He had fully given himself over to believing this could be done. Then, with a smooth motion, he took the largest beaver by the front legs and lifted it past his chest and face, rising with it and lifting it out of the lodge. I clubbed it decisively on the skull, ending its life in an instant. I was surprised by its size and its weight as I lifted it out of the way—fifty pounds, I thought. Four times Raymond repeated this feat, and four more times I gave them a quick death with no suffering.

Raymond didn't climb out of the lodge jubilant. He was stunned and shaken. The old man had a tear in his eye as he helped Raymond pull his gloves over his freezing fingers. ''Per-fec,'' Johnny said.

"I can't believe what I just saw," I said.

"I know," Raymond sputtered. "I've heard my father talk about things kind of like this. He always said that sometimes the animals give their lives willingly to the hunter. But I never really believed it before."

Johnny Raven gutted the beavers right there and tossed their entrails into the water, each time saying the same few words in Slavey as they made a splash. Recovering from his shock, Raymond said, "My father told me what it means when they say that. It means 'Make more beaver.'"

That night Raymond gave the first of the beaver meat to his great-uncle, a big piece of the fatty tail. I could see the quiet pride in both their eyes, to be able to give and receive according to the old tradition.

As Raymond took a piece of the tail, Johnny encouraged me to try it, too, and I did. It was almost all fat and tasted a lot better than I thought it would, kind of like the greasy fat on the baby back ribs I used to eat back in Texas. Raymond started giggling: the fat was running down our faces. To look at us, we didn't have a care in the world.

Now we were wealthy in meat, or at least it felt like we were. We knew better than to ever eat our fill—we didn't know how long it was going to have to last. But it sure felt good having all that beaver meat up in the cache.

In the middle of the night, I happened to waken. The fire had nearly gone out, and Johnny Raven was stoking it, as he did every few hours to keep it alive. I lay awake aching from the nightly ordeal of spending the endless hours on the ground. I kept picturing Raymond, the way his eyes and the eyes of the beaver were locked together. Then my thoughts drifted back as they often did to an image I kept seeing of my father, always looking down out of the window of an airplane.

I was within a moment of falling back asleep when, through my lashes, I saw the white patch of the old man's hair bobbing in the near darkness of the cabin. When I looked again, I saw the dark outline of his body with arms outspread. Johnny was flapping his arms like the wings of a bird. He was standing over Raymond and was taking little hops, both feet at once, hopping and flapping his "wings." He did this dance for several minutes, and then he lay back down in his blanket.

What did it mean, Johnny dancing over Raymond like that? A celebration for what Raymond had done that day? A kind of prayer? I fell back to sleep wondering, knowing I'd seen something Johnny hadn't even meant Raymond to see, much less me.

A foot of new snow fell while Johnny was out moose-hunting the next day. With the beaver meat, we were all eating well enough to get our strength back. Johnny had stretched the beaver pelts on hoops of willow and hung them along the walls. In the evenings he was tanning the pelts with a paste that he made from the brains. He was going to make a pair of oversized mitts for Raymond. With difficulty, he made a joke that the women better not come up to Deadmen Valley and see him doing the tanning. When his hands weren't busy making something, he tapped the drum and told the old stories in his own language. Raymond listened, and he started to try out the Slavey he remembered from school, and to ask for the meaning of other words. Johnny Raven was pleased in his quiet way.

On Christmas Day, Johnny Raven prepared as usual

for his hunt in the morning twilight. Raymond asked if we should go with him. The old man patted him fondly on the shoulder but indicated that he would go alone. We made the circuit of the snares and deadfalls but didn't find anything. We talked about Christmas, and how we didn't have anything to give each other. "Wishes?" I volunteered. "What else do we have?"

"You go first," Raymond said.

I said, "I guess I wish you get home safe to your family and live a long life, big brother."

Raymond smiled and said, "You can't beat that. I wish that you surprise your father by living through this."

When we returned to the cabin just after dark, Johnny wasn't there. "He's always back before dark," Raymond muttered. We set out on his trail, lit brilliantly by a half-moon reflecting off the snow. We found him no more than a mile from the cabin, pitched forward in an unnatural position in the snow. He was frozen stiff.

At first we could only stare, trying to comprehend what had happened. We knew in an instant what this meant for us, and at the same time could hardly begin to imagine the enormity of our loss.

It looked like he'd never even had time to try to get up. "Heart attack?" I wondered aloud.

Raymond didn't answer. He just knelt in the snow beside Johnny, his eyes closed, and then he let out a wail that might have been heard in Nahanni Butte. The tears welled in my own eyes and froze as they ran down my face.

At last Raymond stood, slowly, then picked up the rifle. He turned and stared past me, and he looked lost. "They always told us to learn everything we could from the elders," Raymond said. "We never paid any attention. We thought it was just some crafts that we didn't need anymore. Johnny was trying to show me everything, everything I would need. I never got to tell him that, to thank him. I never got to tell him anything!"

"You said a lot without words," I said, knowing it to be true. "He really cared about you."

As much as we hated to, we knew we had to leave his body there overnight. We covered it with spruce boughs, then retreated to the cabin, numb and full of dread. It was over for us now. We both knew it. There was nothing more to say.

Raymond remained silent for a long time. He stoked the fire; then he stared at the door of the woodstove, his eyes never even blinking. "He should be buried in the ground," Raymond said finally. "But that's impossible."

"What about cremation?"

"You mean burning?" Raymond thought awhile. "I think that would be okay. I think they even used to do it in the old days, before the missionaries. His spirit's not in his body now anyway, so I guess it doesn't matter. The way the elders talk about it, his spirit will stay close for a long time to the places he lived, before it goes on its long journey."

"That's good for us," I said. "If he stays close, I mean."

"Do you think that could be true?" Raymond asked, looking right at me. "About someone's spirit staying around after they're dead?"

"I was seven when my mother died," I said. "The way I think about it, as long as I can remember her, she's still around to help me."

120

In the morning we felled five dead spruce that we found not far from where Johnny had fallen. It took us all day to build a huge platform of dry timber over a core of kindling and split wood. When we were ready, in the late twilight, I could see Raymond was reluctant to do what had to be done: bring Johnny's body. I told him I would do it.

As I approached the body, I was trembling. "Thank you, Johnny Raven," I whispered aloud as I removed the spruce boughs. "You kept us alive. If I'd listened to you in the first place . . ."

I had never touched a dead person before. I tried to keep my mind clear. I needed to do this right. I held my breath and turned him over. His face showed him caught by surprise, with a thought in his eyes that was never finished. It occurred to me that his last thought may have been of us, the fix we'd be in.

My eyes fell on his moccasins. I realized that they could save us if one of us got our feet wet. It was difficult to remove them with his feet frozen solid, but at last I succeeded.

"What else?" I said aloud. "I know you'd want to help us any way you could."

With great difficulty I removed his parka, down vest, and sweater. I noticed that one pocket of his wool shirt was bulging. Inside I found a thick envelope, folded in half and sealed. I stuffed the envelope in my parka pocket and zipped it shut. I checked the rest of his pockets in case there was something else. There was nothing. I saved his belt and the sheath knife that was attached to it.

I lifted his body over my shoulder. It was lighter even than I would have guessed. I was thankful my ribs had mostly healed, and that I still had the strength to carry him. I walked with him through the woods, fear finding my bones worse than the cold ever had.

Raymond was nowhere around, but when I'd placed Johnny's body on the top of the pyre, Raymond appeared out of the trees with a wad of shredded birchbark in his hands. Taking the flint-and-steel fire starter from around his neck, Raymond said, "He really liked this thing. I think it would be good for me to start the fire with this."

Raymond pulled the fire starter apart, roughed up the little white cube with his pocket knife, then propped up shreds of birchbark above the cube. In the darkness, the steel striker made a brilliant shower of sparks, white-hot at the center. Some of the sparks fell on the cube and a flame was born. The flame quickly rose above the cube. Raymond fed the fire with tiny pieces of tinder, then reached in with two little sticks and retrieved the cube. He spit on it to put it out, saying, "Johnny wouldn't want us to waste one of these."

The fire advanced quickly through the tinder and dry sticks. I pulled Raymond back as the big logs caught on fire. The heat was growing dangerously intense. We stepped back even farther. A few minutes later, Johnny's body was going up fast in a column of black smoke.

When the logs began to collapse upon themselves, I tugged at Raymond's parka and said, "He's gone, Raymond. It's you and me now."

We turned away, stopping to collect Johnny's things. Raymond took the sheath knife from the belt and hung it from his own. We started back toward the cabin. From far off we could still hear the popping and crackling of the burning spruce, and when we turned we could see the flames lighting the shaggy trees all around.

Just then the northern lights swept over Deadmen Valley from the mountain rims, streaming and spiraling all around with reds and purples in addition to the greens and yellows I'd seen before. From horizon to horizon the sky was ablaze with magic bonfires. "There's an old story," Raymond said, his voice breaking, "that the northern lights are the spirits of great warriors."

"I like that," I said.

"I don't think Johnny would've wanted to die in a house or a hospital. This way he got to die up the Nahanni, where he was born."

For a while we stood and watched the sparks joining the aurora and the stars. Then we went back inside the cabin and started a fire in the stove. No white-haired Johnny sitting on that third stool and making something with his hands. No Johnny Raven drumming quietly, telling the old stories. The sound of his voice, his language—gone. There was nothing to be said. Both of us were lost in our own thoughts of the dark path that lay ahead.

I remembered the envelope I had taken from Johnny's shirt pocket. I gave it to Raymond, who opened it and took out a neatly typed document. I lit the last candle, already half-gone. Raymond read to himself a bit, then he looked up and said, "It's by the nurse at the hospital. But really it's from him."

"Read it," I said.

14

My name is Mary Canadien,' " Raymond read aloud. " 'I am a nurse at the hospital here in Yellowknife, N.W.T. I am a Dene from Fort Providence. My patient, Johnny Raven, has asked me to write down his testament for him in English as he tells it to me in Slavey. I regret that the English words that follow will only be an approximation of his thoughts in Slavey.' "

Johnny Raven is my name. My last name comes from my original Dene name, which meant Raven's Eye. I was born not far below the great falls of the Nahanni. I was born of the mountain people who lived on the Yukon side of the mountains in the winter and built long boats out of moose skins to come down the Keele River or the Ross or the Nahanni in the spring to trade at the forts. At the end of the summer we would pack our dogs and return on foot to the mountains, where we made our fall hunt, mostly sheep back then.

We made as much dry meat as we could for the winter. We were never many, and the new diseases that were coming into the country took many lives, including my mother's. After that we had to stay in the low country. My father took me to the mission, but I didn't stay there very long. He came back for my little brother and me and we lived in the bush. Sometimes I wish I had stayed longer at the mission, only because I would have learned English there.

As it is, today, I cannot speak with my grandchildren and the other young people, and that is the worst thing. If they understood Slavey, I could tell them the stories and what we learned. Sometimes when I think about their future, I am overwhelmed with sadness. Is it true that what the elders know, the young people no longer need to know? I am leaving my thoughts in hopes that some young person will read them and maybe think about them. I will not live much longer. So this is my message to you.

When we lived in the bush, the land was beautiful and felt just like it was new. We always had to be working to try to survive. We lived in lean-tos and stick teepees covered with branches or hides. Most times there was enough to eat, and there was joking and laughter and dances. We wore rabbit skins, beaver or caribou jackets if we were lucky. But sometimes there was no game, not even rabbits. When I was eleven, my father starved to death.

In 1928 that's when all the people came together to get the treaty payments. They were all in one place when the steamboat came down the Deh Cho and the influenza arrived with it. Many of the elders died, and many of the young, including my first wife, my baby son, and baby daughter.

More and more white men came into the country. They built houses for us if we would stay in the village instead of living out in the bush. It was necessary, they said, so that the children could go to school. So we accepted our payments and the houses that they built for us so that we would live like them, and our children went to school so they would talk like them and think like them.

I have lived in the village for many years now. I am not cold unless I go camping out on the land. I don't ever have to be hungry. I see everyone sitting and watching TV all the time. Some of the best hunters these days have gotten so good at loading up their VCRs they've forgotten how to load their rifles. There are so many useless pursuits now that can't make anyone happy. My mind always goes back to living in the bush and watching the ways of the animals, the sun and the moon and the rivers, and I think that the life we lived on the land was much more interesting.

Outside the village the land is changing. It is not so beautiful as it was. Fewer and fewer animals can live on it. First it was gold and then it was oil, then it was uranium and gold again, then the forests themselves, now it is diamonds. Only a few people benefit, almost never the Dene.

The Dene have never been a greedy people. Just as the bear shares its den with the porcupine, we have shared with others who have come. Now our young people will have to say, "Enough is enough," but unless they know the land they won't fight for it. Unless they think like real Dene people, they won't even have the land to go to anymore when they need it.

There is so much unhappiness among the young people now. Anger . . . drinking . . . fighting . . . They say they are bored, and I believe they are. If I didn't stay busy, always making something, I would be bored, too. We Dene used to roam over the land; there was always something new. The land is all around us, the land has the answers, but many of us don't even go there anymore.

The young people now have it much harder than we ever did. Because who would want to go back at a time when you could starve to death? Yet if they stay in the village and do nothing, they will die inside. They have to go away and get a school education, but away from home they don't have any idea who they are. So they come back to the village, and then they are angrier than before.

They have it much harder. They need education to get good jobs, like this nurse at the hospital. They need to become the carpenters and the mechanics and the teachers. But I believe this, too: they also need a bush education. Otherwise, they won't be happy even if they are successful. They need to get both educations just like they need to learn both languages.

In the old times, when the elders passed on what they had learned to the next generation, it wasn't so we could go back to the past. It was to ensure that the people would know what they needed to continue to survive. That's the way the elders still feel today. We want to help our young people face *the future. If they lose their knowledge of the land and the knowledge of their own language, the real Dene will disappear forever.*

I hope the old stories will not die. They are beautiful. They help us to pass the wisdom down from all the elders who are gone. The elders had strong medicine that was gained from the land and the spirits of the land, and it could be passed down. Myself, I have always had strong raven medicine. I wish I had someone to give it to.

The nurse asks how it's been in the hospital. I say, I miss the taste of moose tongue and beaver tail. I don't know if I will ever taste them again. The doctor wants me to stay here, but as I told him, it's time to go back to Nahanni now.

And so I say to you: take care of the land, take care of yourself, take care of each other.

Johnny Raven

15

We stayed inside the cabin the next day. I was stoking the fire and Raymond was in a trance, holding Johnny's little hand drum and focusing on nothing at all. Outside, the wind down from the arctic was blowing a gale as it almost always did in Deadmen Valley, bending the tall spruces as if they were saplings. The gusts blasted down the frozen river, driving the stinging snow and compressing it into drifts.

In the afternoon Raymond took the letter out and read it over to himself, then folded it back up and stuck it in his pocket. The letter didn't seem to give him any peace. I took the file and sharpened the ax just to have something to do. Raymond never noticed me.

I went down to the creek with the ax to break open the spot where we always collected our water. The entire area was covered with a slowly moving sheet of overflow water that had the consistency of oozing gelatin. The overflow was coming from just upstream, where a strong head of water was bubbling up through the ice like an artesian well. As Raymond had explained to me, when the creeks freeze deep, the water moving under the ice has to find somewhere to go, so it splits the ice at a weak point and forces its way to the surface, where it fans out in a slushy mass before freezing solid.

Above the source of the overflow I found a new collection spot and accidentally splashed water all over myself trying to chop the new hole. The water froze instantly to my clothes; I barely noticed. I was in a sort of trance myself. I hauled the water back to the cabin. I made what we were calling beaver stew, with no other ingredients but shredded beaver meat and water. All the while my mind was racing. I had only one thought: escape down the frozen Nahanni while we still had food and strength. There had never been another airplane. We'd quietly given up on the signal fire at least ten days ago. We had to do something. The two brothers this valley was named after—the prospectors back in 1908—didn't get out in time.

I handed Raymond a plate of beaver stew. He looked at me as if he'd never been away, and he said, "We have to get out of here."

"Amen to that," I agreed. "And before it snows again—a lot of snow would make it a whole lot harder. Hike out down the river, is that what you're thinking, too?"

With a nod, he said, "There's no other way. We only have two bullets left. We don't have any reason to think the moose are still around, and even if they were, I can't hunt like Johnny. Let's go while we still have the beaver meat."

"If we come to open water, we'll just walk around it. How far is it down to Nahanni Butte, do you think?"

"Too far to carry the meat and everything on our backs. It could be a hundred miles, and who knows how long it would take us. We need to make a toboggan."

"Is it canyon all the way?"

"The last forty miles or so is all different. It's called the Splits—that's where I got my moose. The river winds all over the place. It's got lots of islands, lots of different channels. All open country, real flat."

We found two perfectly straight young birches on a ridge three or four hundred feet above the floor of the valley. We prepared the logs just as Johnny had, stripping long slats for the toboggan the same way he'd stripped material for the snowshoe frames. Then we went to work with my pocketknife and Raymond's sheath knife, whittling our narrow boards down to roughly uniform thickness.

Raymond slowly worked the bend into the slats at one end, shaping them over his knee. We lashed them together with babiche and tied the curved front end back to the toboggan to keep the proper bend in place while the wood was drying out. The toboggan took us three days to build. As we were finishing it, I scooped up a handful of shavings and was about to toss them in the stove. Raymond said, "Maybe we shouldn't do that."

"Why not?"

"The elders always take the scraps outside and spread them out in the woods. They say otherwise you won't find a good birch when you need one."

I thought about it and said, "There might be something to that."

"I guess it's showing respect for a tree. They always say even the trees have spirits. Sounds crazy, I guess."

I said, "If I'd never been to the North, maybe it would sound crazy to me. But I'm getting the idea. It's like 'Make more beaver.'"

When I said that he added, "They say that living

things don't die right away when they're killed or cut down. The spirit can stay around for days or months or even longer.''

"Same as our old friend," I pointed out.

We used the bowline I'd salvaged from the raft as the pull-rope for the toboggan. It was all we had left of the parachute cord. We attached it at both ends on the front. One of us would pull the toboggan by walking inside the rope.

On the last day of the year we precooked all the beaver meat for our hike out. It was Raymond's idea. The easy part was the quick-freezing: set your plates of stew outside the door, wait ten minutes, then chuck the rations into the army box. The meat filled one box and half of the second one.

Sometime during our last night in the cabin, a bird started croaking, not very far away. "Did you hear that?" Raymond whispered.

"Raven?"

"Ravens aren't supposed to talk at night. . . . That's not a good sign."

In the morning twilight we decided on what was absolutely essential. Everything else we'd leave behind. We'd take along Johnny's moccasins and his blanket. We'd leave most of the pots and pans, Raymond's gym shoes, the camp shovel, Johnny's parka, the beautiful beaver pelts he had tanned. Raymond looked a long time at Johnny's hand drum, then said, "I'll come back for this next summer."

We lashed everything down on the toboggan, including all three pairs of snowshoes. We rigged the ax where we could get at it. Raymond shouldered the packsack, latched the door, and picked up the rifle. I started out pulling the toboggan and had the daypack on my back. It was New Year's Day and forty degrees below zero. That's seventy-two degrees below freezing, I thought. I took a glance back at the cabin and saw the blue smoke drifting out of the chimney and spreading out along the ground. I remembered the night Johnny had led us to this cabin, under the northern lights, and I thought about all that had happened there. Raymond, I realized, was also looking back.

The surface of the Nahanni was mostly glare ice. The toboggan was sliding along behind me of its own accord. The walking was so easy we soon rounded an island, passed a second, and found ourselves about where our log raft had piled against the ice a month before. Not far ahead loomed the tall gate of the lower canyon. A short while later we entered the gate and passed inside.

A couple of miles and around a bend, we encountered an icy fog hugging the bottom of the canyon. It had to be coming from open water. Raymond and I looked at each other and said nothing. Forty below zero, yet open water, just as we had feared.

When we got down to the riffles, our fears eased. It was only a narrow strip of running water, with a cliff on the left but plenty of room to get around on the right.

Every mile or two we encountered another stretch of open water. I couldn't understand it. Right beside the exposed water, the ice would be a full two feet thick. "I don't get it," I said. "Why isn't the ice two feet thick all across the river? What causes these open spots? It's January!"

"It beats me," Raymond said. "Maybe tricky currents can rile up the water and keep it from freezing."

"That might explain it."

"Maybe there's even hot springs right under the bed of the river. I know about some farther down—I've been there, right where the canyon ends and the Splits begins."

We pushed on between the blue-gray walls of the canyon. The rim of the canyon thousands of feet above glowed pink, signaling day's end coming soon, and we thought better of continuing. On an island we cut down a pair of dead spruces and tried to start a fire with the butane lighter, but it wouldn't function at these temperatures. We were out of kitchen matches, so it was going to be Raymond's fire starter from now on. It worked like a charm. By the light of the fire we slashed dead limbs from live trees and dragged in driftwood until we knew we had enough to take us through the night.

A quick supper, two plates apiece; then we got into our sleeping bags and began the torturous wait for those five hours of daylight to return. We sat up into the night stoking the fire, trying to stay as warm as possible. Raymond said, "I wish we could've been at Nahanni Butte for Christmas—you wouldn't believe the food."

"Try me."

Raymond's face glowed. "After church, there's a great big potlatch—a feast. Everybody comes. It's in the community hall."

"How many people is that?"

"Oh, about eighty-five, I guess."

"You're kidding! I was picturing it more like three or four hundred."

He tossed a big branch on the fire. "That's the good thing about Nahanni—everybody knows you. Everybody looks out for everybody else."

"Tell me about the feast," I said. "That's the part I want to know about."

"Well, there's everything you could think of—modern food and traditional. People always save bear meat for potlatches—black bear—with great big straps of fat. That's my favorite."

"When will the next potlatch come along?"

"There'll be one for Johnny, a real big one. People will come from all over. They'll tell about the things he did in his life, and they'll feed his spirit by putting some food in the fire."

"I can picture you doing all that in person," I said. "You'll be there. We're going to make it."

"I could tell about what he did in the very last part of his life."

We slept as best we could, on the blue tarp spread over four inches of branches. Every few hours we'd start shaking, and one of us would get up and heap another round of fuel on the glowing mass of coals.

The next day the wind quit blowing down the canyon, the sky turned a dark gray, and the temperature rose to ten below. The walls of the canyon climbed sheer from the river in some places; in others they rose from slopes of shattered rock. The walls were composed of horizontal bands of limestone from river to sky, like the bluffs along the Guadalupe River back in the Texas hill country but on a grand scale, with dwarf evergreens clinging to impossible locations and frozen waterfalls attached to sheer rock faces and glowing pale blue.

Every time we encountered open water we found a way around one side or the other. Our hopes were soaring. "We'll be taking a bath in those hot springs soon," Raymond said.

135

"Instead of a sponge bath without a sponge."

Late in the day we passed an island with the typical massive driftpile on its upstream end. We talked about camping there, but islands and driftpiles were plentiful and an hour of twilight remained. We decided to press on. Raymond was pulling the toboggan, and I had the packsack on my back.

Just below the island, where the canyon narrowed, open water rushed out from under the ice and sped toward a cliff on the left side, leaving no ice to walk on over there. From the cliff, the strip of open water angled gradually back across the entire width of the river, passing briefly under a big ice bridge before splashing against another sheer cliff a short distance down on the right side of the canyon. "Bad luck," I said. "Open water from cliff to cliff."

We were stopped. Unless we wanted to try crossing on the ice bridge.

I looked downriver. If we got past this place, it was good walking as far as I could see. We approached the ice bridge and took a closer look. It was about fifty feet across and about ten to twenty feet wide, with ice shelves extending to the shores on either side.

"What do you think?" I asked Raymond. "It looks to me like it should hold us. . . ."

Raymond kept studying the bridge. "Could we build a raft and get across here? There's that driftpile we just passed."

"We don't have any parachute cord, except for the pull-rope on the toboggan, and that sure wouldn't do it. I don't know, maybe we could tear some of our stuff into strips to tie the logs together."

"I don't know either," Raymond said slowly. "The

water's so fast. . . . Even if we could patch together some kind of raft tomorrow, we'd have to launch it just past the ice bridge, and from there it's such a short distance on the water—fifty meters maybe? Then the raft would crash against the cliff at the bottom, and we'd be scrambling to get out on the ice. What if the ice down there wouldn't hold us?''

"It'll all be happening real fast," I said. "That's for sure."

"It's getting so late," Raymond said, looking around. "I think fooling with a raft would be riskier than the ice bridge. We sure could waste a lot of time and wreck our stuff trying it."

Dropping the packsack to the ground, I took off my parka and cap, my outer mitts, and then my gloves, and tucked them under the lashing on the toboggan. I started for the ice bridge. "I'll test it first without all this stuff on."

"Careful, Gabe."

I took a few steps onto the ice bridge. "So far, so good," I said. "I think it's okay."

"Are you sure?" I heard from behind me.

"Slow and easy," I said, taking a few more steps. I glanced back and saw Raymond there watching intently.

Halfway across, with no warning, the ice broke with a sudden crack. I spun around, trying to get back to safety, but the big middle piece of the bridge under me slumped and broke free into the river. As I struggled for balance, the mass of ice started floating downriver with me on it. I looked over and saw Raymond on the shore, saw the shock on his face. Then I looked downstream and realized exactly what was going to happen.

If I floated past that cliff on the right, Raymond couldn't possibly reach me. Just as I realized I was going to have to swim for it, the ice underneath me rolled and I was pitched into the water.

Now you've done it, I thought. The shock of the cold water squeezed all the breath out of my lungs. I caught a glimpse of Raymond running along the bank. All encumbered by my heavy clothes and boots, I swam as best I could for the shore. I had to get to the shore before the cliff or I was dead.

I concentrated on Raymond's face inside that circle of fur on his parka ruff. The wall was coming up fast. I swam with all the strength I had left, fighting the clothes and the boots. I thought I'd lost, but his arm reached out and yanked me out of the water and onto the ice.

"Get up!" he was yelling.

Get up . . . ? I couldn't even breathe. He stood me up, and my clothes stiffened just that fast. He hustled me along the shore, stopping only to pull on my parka, mitts, and cap. "We need fire!" he shouted, and started yanking the toboggan upriver. "We got to get back to that driftpile!"

I ran alongside thinking, Now you've done it! Now you've done it! I kept stumbling forward encased in my ice-hardened clothes, losing the feeling in my arms and legs. I could see the driftpile now in the dimming twilight. All pumped up with adrenaline, I ran ahead of Raymond.

When we got to the driftpile I kept running back and forth, just trying to keep moving. I was aware of Raymond gathering kindling; I saw him take shredded birchbark out of his pocket. I saw the shower of sparks from his fire starter. I watched his kindling catch, I rushed over, he pushed me back. He was adding more sticks, babying his fire. I was standing there frozen as a post, brain frozen, too. Raymond turned to the toboggan, freed the tarp, threw the spare clothes on it, including Johnny Raven's moccasins.

The wind was fanning the fire into the heart of the driftpile. It was dry wood, and it went up fast. I stood close, too close—Raymond yelled at me to get back, and he helped me strip off my wet clothes.

The driftpile was becoming an inferno of heat. Within another five minutes I was flash cooked. I changed into dry clothes, pulled on Johnny's moccasins. The flames soared twenty, thirty feet high, pushing us farther and farther back and lighting up the canyon walls hundreds of feet above.

The danger was over, no damage done. Raymond nodded toward the bonfire. "It's not a hot spring, but same idea."

"You saved my life," I said.

Raymond waved me off. "Oh, I just didn't want to go back to Deadmen Valley by myself."

In the morning we started back to the cabin. We were beaten, quiet as the canyon itself and filled with dread. It warmed up and began to snow about midday. By the next morning, three feet of snow had fallen. We took turns breaking trail and muscling the toboggan. My ribs started aching again. My mind drifted away from the effort and the tedium of lifting one snowshoe high, then the next, while pulling the toboggan. I figured out that the brothers who ended up headless back in 1908 probably had tried to escape down the river, just like we had, and they'd been turned back to Deadmen Valley, just like we had.

The return trip took us four days, slogging through the deep snow. At last the cabin came into sight and we trudged the last hundred yards, completely spent. I took off my snowshoes, unlatched the cabin door, and was nearly inside when I detected a quick movement in the back of the cabin. I caught a glimpse of wreckage and became aware of a strong, repulsive smell as my eyes found my danger: in a back corner behind sections of stovepipe and the upended table crouched a dark, heavily furred animal I'd never seen before in my life, about the size of a small bear. Its beady eyes were locked on mine. Then it bared its teeth.

Suddenly the cabin erupted with a vicious, snarling, utterly ferocious growl. Just then Raymond grabbed my parka and yanked me back, yelling, "Wolverine!"

Raymond pulled me back outside through the open door, shouting, "He'll tear your face off!"

Barely behind us, the wolverine shot out the door. It ran halfway across the clearing, then stopped and looked back at us, still growling. I got a good look at the long front claws and powerful jaws. "They're not that big," Raymond said, "but even grizzlies leave 'em alone."

In another moment the nasty-tempered, low-slung little beast loped off into the forest with a strange, bounding gait.

"How'd he get in?" I wondered aloud.

We stepped back inside the cabin. The place smelled rank, worse than musky. My question was answered as I looked up to see a hole in the roof where the wolverine had torn out the roof jack and knocked the stovepipe apart.

Just about everything we'd left behind was in tatters. Raymond reached for Johnny's drum, which had been slashed into shreds.

16

It was one hundred and ten degrees warmer inside the cabin than outside. It was the seventh of January. Outside, trees were splitting open from the extreme cold, making a sound like gunshots. My breath made a crackling sound when it hit the air. The cold had Deadmen Valley in its grip, and its grip felt crushing and malicious. Fifty degrees below zero, midday, yet we had to go out and make firewood. Fifty below felt to me about twice as cold as twenty below, much more dense and much more penetrating. It hushed the land, took the breath out of it and us too. It poured right through all the layers we were wearing and into our bones.

Yet we were thinking about leaving the warmth of the cabin.

One of those army boxes stuffed full of beaver meat, that was all we had left. It won't be much longer until it's over, I thought. It was Raymond who brought up the Yukon. He said, "Johnny's letter said the mountain Dene used to spend the winter over on the Yukon side of these mountains."

"What are you getting at?" I asked.

142

"They spent the winter over there because the animals leave this side and go over there. The people had to follow the animals."

"That makes sense," I murmured.

"Back when we were camped above the falls, Johnny told us there wouldn't be game down here. He knew they all leave. I think his letter tells us the only thing we can do now."

"You mean hike to the Yukon?"

"We have two rifle shells. We could get a moose over there if we're lucky."

"Where is the Yukon?"

"To the west," he said. "Over those mountains. When we get a moose, we'll make a brush teepee right there, and spend the rest of the winter. One moose would get us through till breakup. The Beaver River is over there on the Yukon side—it flows into the Liard. With the moose hide, we could make enough babiche to lash together a raft and float all the way down to Nahanni Butte."

A blizzard pinned us in the cabin for the next four days, but we needed the time to get ready for the cold that Raymond said was yet to come. With needles and an awl from the sewing kit and fishing line from the tackle box, but mostly with determination, Raymond put together a pair of huge beaver-fur mitts for himself from the pelts Johnny had tanned, several of which had survived the wolverine rampage.

While the snow fell, I made hooded face masks for both of us from Johnny's red blanket, with openings for eyes, nose, and mouth. Whenever a lull in the storm came along, I went out on the snowshoes and rounded up birchbark for tinder in case we couldn't find any where we were going.

Finally the storm was over. Pulling my cap down over my ears, I joined Raymond outside and latched the door behind me. Deadmen Valley, cloaked with deep snow, lay breathless and still. The cottonwoods along the river were all rimmed with frost, and they looked like ghosts of trees. The temperature was back up to twenty-five degrees below zero. We shoed up; I pulled on my big mitts over my gloves and stepped inside the sled's pull-rope. Raymond led, carrying the packsack and breaking trail. I threw my weight against the rope and we took off, this time without looking back. We walked into utter silence, and the silence closed behind us as we passed.

We'd decided to stay out of the streambeds as much as we could, in order to avoid the places where overflow could be hiding, where the water down in the streambed had burst up through the ice and lay hidden as slush below the snow. We were going to try to escape the valley by climbing directly for the gap between the bald mountain and its nearest neighbor to the southwest— everything else was too straight up and down. We had to hope that the gap would lead us over the mountains and into the Yukon, where the moose winter. As I trudged forward I kept saying to myself, "One moose, that's all we need. One moose. Raymond's moose."

The new snow had no crust and no bottom to it. Trading off with the toboggan, we waded through it, lifting our legs high to raise the tips of our snowshoes. It cost us a huge expenditure of energy. The temperature dropped, and the trees once again started going off like pistol shots. Despite all the protection, my feet ached with the cold, and my fingers too. The wind began to blow, searing our chins and noses, so they burned and went numb. We stopped and pulled on our masks. I envied the small animals who'd left their tracks atop the snow: squirrels and snowshoe hares as well as the marten, fox, and lynx that were stalking them.

We made our camp on a ridge several thousand feet above the floor of the valley and halfway to the bald mountain. The wind died away and the first stars came out, and with them the northern lights, spiraling around and waving their neon tentacles. Though we were exhausted and dehydrated, we built a low lean-to, floored it with spruce boughs, covered it with the blue tarp, and heaped snow on top, using our snowshoes for shovels. The prospect of a fire's warmth kept us going, along with the thought of something hot to eat and the chance to melt snow and produce all the water we could drink. The only water storage we had during the day was one liter each in our water bottles, which we carried inside our parkas so it wouldn't freeze.

The wind blew hard all night, but we discovered in the morning that it had done us a favor, crusting the snow into slabs that mostly supported our snowshoes on top of the snowpack. We kept climbing, searing our lungs, climbing, taking turns with the toboggan.

When we stopped to look back, we could see the Nahanni snaking through the entire expanse of Deadmen Valley between the upper and lower canyons. The river was frozen and white except for that one small patch of open water that even now refused to freeze. Across the river the valley speared up against a world of peaks pure white above the timberline. I said to Raymond, "I can't believe where we are."

"Where we are in the middle of the winter," he replied. "I never would've believed this in a million years. Only the old people like Johnny ever saw this in the winter."

"It's amazing they could survive."

"They say our people have been living here for thousands of years. Before rifles, before modern clothes, before hardly anything. They had to know *everything* about the land."

"You know more than you think, Raymond."

He spit, and the spit froze before it reached the ground. "I don't know anything. I was starting to learn stuff out on the trapline with my dad, but after I was about ten I quit going out with him."

At the end of the day we made our camp at timberline, and the following morning we passed through the gap of the shoulder of the bald mountain. That mountain turned out to be only a buttress on the rim of a vast plateau above the treeline. At ten-thirty in the morning the sun rose brilliant and blinding, the first time we'd laid eyes on it in weeks. We'd climbed so high we were able to enjoy the sun for several hours as it crept toward our Yukon divide to the southwest.

We followed the edge of the plateau, using the compass when we couldn't use the sun. Before long we were able to take off our snowshoes. Up here, with no tree cover, the wind had blown most of the snow away, leaving no more than a couple of hardened inches.

Within a few miles we came across a place where animals had dug in the snow to get at the grass. "Dall sheep," Raymond said. The rest of the day we kept seeing their tracks, finding their droppings and the places they'd scratched in the snow to expose the grass. "Looks like they were here not so long ago," Raymond said.

"Do you think we should try to get a sheep?" I asked.

"Not enough meat. We've got to get a moose."

We camped in a dark finger of timber that reached up into the plateau. It took us an hour to find enough firewood. Then we dug snow where it had drifted so we could melt it for drinking water. After we got some hot water into us we cooked our supper. In the extreme cold, we'd gone from one meal a day to two. It was nearly the dark of the moon, yet we could still get around by the light of an infinity of stars reflecting off the snow. The aurora, bright overhead, seemed to be dancing a figure eight around the Big Dipper and the North Star. I realized that I hadn't seen the contrail of a single jet across the sky for months.

I tried to go to sleep, but sleep never came easily with the cold seeping through the sleeping bag and all the layers of my clothing as if it were a liquid. I was looking at Orion the Hunter and I was thinking of Johnny. Suddenly wolves broke loose in a wavering chorus. Their howling seemed to come right out of the black spaces between the stars. Thinking about what was to come, I felt scared, really scared. The howling kept up, and seemed to strike the same inhuman chord as the subarctic night.

Over the course of the endless night I saw the high, transparent cirrus clouds race under a sliver of a moon, felt the wind kicking up, saw the thicker clouds come in and snuff out the moon altogether. The snow began to fall even before the morning twilight. Fortunately, we were sheltered by the stunted trees around us, but still, the swirling winds were blowing some of the stinging snow into our lean-to.

When twilight arrived, the storm only intensified. "Could be a blizzard," Raymond said.

That's exactly what it turned out to be, but a better word for it was *misery*. All that time, in the teeth of the storm, we had to keep scavenging for any kind of wood that would burn. Without the trees, stunted and pitiful as they were, we would've been dead. Our fire seemed to do so little to warm us. But we had to keep melting snow for water, and we had to eat. Our meat was going fast.

I kept track of the days on my watch. The fourteenth of January gave way to the fifteenth and the sixteenth. Out on the plateau, just a few feet away from the trees, it was an all-white world without references of any kind. Midday on the sixteenth, the sun came out. "Think we should go for it?" I asked, all out of patience, but Raymond shook his head. "If there's more coming," he said, "and it catches us out in the open, we might not even be able to see each other."

In another hour the storm was back. If and when we got going again, I didn't really believe we were going to get a moose. We'd just be slogging our way to oblivion.

The blizzard lasted another day. When we finally started out, I put on a good face. "Let's go find your moose!" I said to Raymond. The look he gave me didn't exactly echo my pretended optimism. Though the new snow was crusted and forgiving for snowshoes, both of us seemed to be drained of the mental stamina it would take to keep going. We were following the rim of the plateau west and keeping our bearings on the divide in the distance, but it never seemed to get any closer. I felt like a walking dead man, all out of hope and going on reflex. Finally Raymond quit walking, slumped on the toboggan. "I can't do this," he said. "It's pointless."

"Don't worry, Raymond," I said. "You'll find the moose."

With his heavy mitt, he swiped at the ice buildup around the mouth-hole of his mask. "I'm not Johnny Raven!" he cried out.

For several minutes I couldn't speak. I didn't know what to say. "Just keep trying," I pleaded finally. "Just don't give up."

"Our meat will never hold out until we get a moose."

All I could think of to say was "We have to keep trying."

"You . . . you never even complain!"

"Neither do you," I answered him, and it was true. "I'll tell you, though, if you want to get me started, I feel like I've been pulled through six knotholes and poked in the eye with a sharp stick."

With a weak smile, he said, "That makes me feel better."

Late in the day we came across the fresh tracks of sheep, and of wolves that had walked in their trail. The tracks led down off the rim onto a bench pointing back to the east. "It's not the direction we're going," Raymond said, "but we have to get some more meat. If we're ever going to get a moose, we have to keep eating."

"One bullet for a sheep and one for a moose?" I asked. "Is that what you're thinking?"

With a shrug, he said, "I think that's what Johnny would do."

We came down off the plateau and along the foot of a long line of cliffs pocked with caves, following the trail of the sheep and wolves. Raymond stopped at a particular spot, I didn't know why. I sagged, panting. Raymond stood there a long time eyeing the cliff and a cavern perched about thirty feet above us. Then he said, "Sheep went up there. Look," he said, pointing, "right there the moss is torn off."

At first I couldn't see a thing. I looked harder. Yes, I could see it now, the torn pieces of moss. I could even see a few droppings on the route the sheep had taken to get up to the cave.

"Wolves can't climb that," Raymond said, suddenly intense. "That's why the sheep go up there. After the wolves leave, the sheep can come down. But there's a chance some are still up there where we can't see them."

"Then let's go find out," I said.

Raymond climbed first with the rifle. I scrambled up behind him. No sheep in sight, only an opening fifty feet wide and just as high, but there were plenty of droppings, some of them fresh. Sheep had indeed milled around here on the lip of the cave. "You were right," I said.

The footing was treacherous. The water falling from seeps high above had built up a sheet of solid ice that inclined back toward the inside of the cavern. We inched forward until we could begin to see down and into the murkiness. The ice made a continuous slope that suddenly pitched down like a crystal slide to the floor of the cave twenty feet below. I thought I saw something move. I looked again. Standing there looking up at us from the darkness was a white sheep. A single white sheep. It was a big ram, quite alive and apparently in good condition, with tremendous, curling horns.

17

The ram was standing amid the skulls and skeletons of sheep that must have starved to death in this cave over the centuries. "Can we get him out of there once you shoot him?" I wondered aloud.

"Slide down just like he did, then chop stairs back up with the ax," Raymond said with a smile on his face, the first in a long time. The ram just stood there, looking up at us.

Raymond lay down on his belly with the rifle. He took aim and focused all his concentration. I'm sure the cold metal touching his bare hand burned like fire. I was just hoping that the ram didn't make a sudden move. I expected the blast of the rifle at any instant.

Instead of firing, Raymond set the rifle down and reached for his glove. "Wait a minute," he said, looking up at me. "Maybe we don't have to shoot him. Maybe we can get him with the ax, and save this bullet."

"Of course!" I said. "What a great idea! Should I slide down into the cave?"

"Let's think some more abut how we're going to do it. This sheep isn't going anywhere. Let's find camp, start a fire, eat some food, get some rest."

We climbed back down the cliff. A hundred yards farther along the base of the cliff we found another cave and made camp there. That evening we each ate three plates of stew. In the morning we ate three more, nearly finishing our rations.

The ram was lying down when it saw us appear. It stood, looking up at us. We took off our masks—they were such a hindrance. I slid down first, avoiding the scattered skulls and bones. The ram retreated into the poor light at the back of the cave, squared off, and lowered his head, fronting those huge horns. The cave had a faint sweetness to its musty air, an ancient residue of death. "The ax," I called up to Raymond, wondering if the ram might charge me.

The ram stayed put as I began to chop out our stairs back up. When I finished the last step and joined Raymond at the top, the ram ran back into the light, stared up at us, and gave a snort. "Killing this ram might not be so easy," I said, "even with the two of us."

"You're right." Raymond nodded. "He could hurt us bad with those horns before we could get a swing at him."

"How 'bout a lasso?" I suggested. "We could take apart the pull-rope on the toboggan."

When the time came, the ram skittered back and forth across the dusty floor of the cave a couple of times, then froze at the back in the near darkness to face us. I had the lasso ready, but aiming was going to be difficult. I crept closer, knowing the ram was thinking about charging. If he did, I was going to get behind Raymond and his ax real fast.

A half-dozen times my crude lasso came close, striking the ram's horns but falling to the ground. At last it settled over the horns and I cinched it down fast. "You got him," I heard Raymond exclaim.

The ram bolted from the back of the cave, away from both of us, and I held on tight. Suddenly I lost my footing, went down hard, and was being dragged across the floor of the cave. I saw the ram kicking at the rope, fighting it, then he tripped up and went down, hoofs and horns flailing all over the place as Raymond came down on him with the dull butt of the axhead, again and again.

Shuddering, the ram was in his death throes. When I looked up at Raymond, I saw that he had taken a deep gash in his forehead and was bleeding all over his parka. He had his hand up against his head, trying to stop the blood. "Hoof got me," he explained as I picked myself up.

"Look at all this meat," he said, freeing his sheath knife. He bent over the ram and bled it at the throat.

"Let's take care of you first," I insisted. "Your forehead is bleeding pretty good."

We got the blood stopped with Raymond's bandanna, then climbed out and returned to camp. I boiled some water and cleaned his wound, about three-quarters of an inch long. Raymond didn't want me to try stitching it up. "No way you're putting a needle in my forehead," he said. "Not without an anesthetic." I used a couple of butterfly bandages on it and then taped down a gauze dressing over that. "Good work, cowboy," he told me when I was done. "Let's go get that sheep."

Our feast began with two smoking-hot sheep kidneys that Raymond insisted couldn't be wasted. We decided to stay for a few days, eat all we wanted, and get our strength back.

The next day we made an interesting discovery about our cave. The front edge of its floor was a rubbish heap of bones and broken arrow points. We figured out that the blacking on the walls of the cave must have come from the smoke of countless prehistoric cooking fires. Raymond's ancestors knew this place well, we decided, and had camped here to take advantage of the sheep that fell down the slide in the neighboring cave.

A raven sailed by, eyeing us at close range. Raymond threw a few scraps to it. It came close within ten or twelve feet, taking the food, watching us with a cold black eye. Raymond fed it all it wanted. The big bird did a few hops, both feet at once, then it flew away croaking, wingtips thrashing the heavy air.

I asked Raymond how it ever happened that he had stopped at the spot where the sheep climb to the cavern, and figured it all out. "I heard a raven flying around up there," he said. "I think the raven could see the sheep."

"Did you see the raven?"

With a shake of his head, he said, "It was weird. I looked for it, but I couldn't see it. I only heard its wings."

After two days, with our strength returning, we knew we had to set out again and try to find a moose. Our breath made those crackling sounds again as it hit the air. It was fifty-five degrees below zero when we left the cave. We had to go slow in order to avoid getting our clothes damp from exertion. At this temperature we couldn't afford any mistakes, and yet we had to try to get over the mountains and into the Yukon. Raymond mentioned that his father always said it was okay to be out in the cold working on the trapline "until nothing was moving in the woods."

"Does it get this cold down at Nahanni Butte?" I asked. "At the village?"

"Sometimes, but we don't even play street hockey when it gets this cold."

"Does your father still run his trapline?"

"Two years ago he got the job keeping the diesel generator going. It makes the electricity for Nahanni Butte. He's a great mechanic—that's how I learned how to fix snowmobiles."

Other than the occasional rifle-shot crack of a tree freezing and splitting, complete silence reigned in the woods, a profound stillness without even the suggestion of wind. The only sound was that of a raven sometimes overhead, its ragged wingtips beating the dense air.

The snowpack had set up like iron, and the snowshoes gave us complete freedom on it. Raymond's frosty breath ahead of me made fog that swirled around his head and hung in his wake. Squirrels were still moving around in the trees, and sometimes we walked right up on snowshoe hares without seeing them until they suddenly darted away.

The waxing moon rode high in the sky, lighting our way for hours after twilight was gone. It was so bright, reflecting off the snow, I could have read a book by it. The mountain ranges stood out with amazing clarity as they shone in the moonlight, their countless jagged peaks rising from an all-white world that floated high above the dark forests.

I would have thought that the moon would hug the winter horizon in the North, like the sun does, but its arc carried it above the highest mountains. We benefited from it, putting on the miles. The northern lights would come and go, swirling and dancing and shape-shifting. They made me think of Johnny Raven. Sometimes I thought I heard a sound that accompanied them, like humming synthesizer music, and I guessed it was some sort of natural phenomenon associated with the lights, but then I decided it was only my mind playing tricks.

We were traveling through an unworldly dimension, yet it wasn't dreamed.

Raymond and I almost never spoke. It felt like we both knew we were marching toward those black spaces between the stars. As I pulled the toboggan it helped to let my mind drift, having long conversations with my father. I lost all touch with Raymond, who must have been having conversations of his own in his head. Who with? His parents? His brother and sisters? Johnny Raven?

Hike, make shelter, get firewood, melt snow for drinking water, eat, try to get snatches of sleep while you weren't fighting the cold or feeding the fire. Nothing could be accomplished without immense effort and the pain that reminded us we were still alive. The sheep steaks came out of the sack hard as bricks. To keep up our strength, we ate all we could. We no longer had the will to ration ourselves.

On our third day out of the cave we crested the mountains at a wide pass and paused to get our bearings. We had to be looking into the Yukon and the headwaters of the Beaver River on the other side, because as far as we could see, the land sloped down and away into a long river valley. We were both standing there, gasping for breath after the searing climb. Raymond looked up like he saw something, and then his eyes went to the rocky ridgeline up above us along the divide. After a minute he said to me, "That raven . . ."

I was still panting like a worn-out packhorse. All I could think about was how good it was going to feel to start on the long downhill. I hadn't seen a raven.

"Didn't you see that raven?" Raymond asked, his voice hoarse. His face was hidden behind the red mask, which was iced around the mouth and nose holes. His eyelashes had partially frozen together. His lips, like mine, were cracked and caked with dried blood.

I shook my head. "Nope."

"It flew right by, a minute ago. It tucked and rolled right in front of us. Then it flew over to that tree, way over there, the one by itself up in those rocks. It's still there."

Panting, he pointed out the tree, but I still couldn't see the bird. Ravens are big and black. The tree was quite a distance off. I squinted, trying to make out a raven. "I can't quite see it," I said, but I wondered if his mind was playing tricks on him. "Sorry," I said. "I just can't see it."

"You didn't hear it either? It called, *Ggaagga* . . . *ggaagga*—'Animal . . . animal.' "

I shook my head. "I was daydreaming. I've heard so many ravens, maybe I just tuned it out."

"We'd have to do a lot more climbing to go up there," Raymond said.

What was he talking about? Climbing way up on that ridge? After a raven?

For a second I thought I was going to lose it, blow up at him in utter frustration. I held on. I waited. I caught my breath. He'd never blown up at me.

I looked down into the Yukon side all laid out before

158

us, its mountains worn down and subdued compared to all the jagged ranges behind us. It was more important to stick by Raymond than to make sense. "You're our hunter," I said. "You should call it. Even if it doesn't work out—I could use the exercise."

He laughed. A laugh was a scarce commodity.

I said, "I feel as strong as a half-dead musk-ox."

Despite his mask, I could detect a weak smile. Raymond said, "You *are* a musk-ox, little brother."

We struggled up the ridgeline to the wind-twisted spruce where Raymond's raven had landed. No raven in sight. "Maybe I'm going crazy," Raymond said.

Now what? I thought. Here we were at the absolute screaming dead end of nowhere.

Still perplexed, Raymond was looking all around for his raven. At last his gaze fixed on a narrow gap through the divide ahead of us and several hundred feet below. "I see blood on the snow," he said.

I squinted hard. I thought I saw some spots of bright red. "I think you're right," I said.

I followed him down to the gap. We found a trail of blood and the tracks of a moose. Alongside the tracks of the moose, the tracks of wolves. I knelt to touch the blood, to tell myself I wasn't imagining all of this.

It was real.

"Look at this," Raymond said. He was pointing to large bird tracks in the snow. Raven tracks.

I shook my head, trying to add it all up. I couldn't. The important thing was, here was the trail of a moose.

The blood trail had come from the Yukon side and was leading down into the headwaters of the stream that flowed off the divide into Deadmen Valley.

"Raymond," I said, "I don't get it how you saw and heard that raven."

"He's a trickster," Raymond replied, as if that explained everything.

Then I remembered something. "In Johnny's letter," I said, "remember how he said he had strong raven medicine and wanted to pass it on?"

"I remember."

"The night before he died, it was the middle of the night and I couldn't sleep. I saw him standing over you, arms out wide like wings, making these little hops like the raven was making that you were feeding back in the cave."

Raymond looked away, and then he murmured, "Raven medicine."

"You never saw the raven when you found the sheep?"

"I only heard its wings."

"Strange stuff," I said.

Raymond pulled his water bottle from inside his parka and took a slow drink. "I don't know what's going on," he said finally. "Maybe all that medicine stuff the old guys talk about, they didn't make it up. Out here, everything's different from the way it is in town."

"Should we go after this moose?"

"It's a fresh trail. . . . Who knows when we'd find another one? We could take it away from the wolves. Wolves are afraid of people."

For two days we followed the blood trail, using the moon to keep up, as it was approaching full. When it had some size to it, the moon was up practically around the clock, and high in the sky—"Like the sun is, in the

160

summer," Raymond explained. We didn't dare to leave off pursuit to camp, cook, eat, or sleep.

It had warmed up to thirty-five below, a tolerable temperature compared to what we had experienced. My feet and fingers didn't ache so badly. The sun, when it made its appearance, was copper-colored and hazy, with a ring around it. Raymond said that meant another cold spell was coming, a deeper, longer cold spell. We paused only to chop holes in the creeks and boil water. Drinking cold water or eating snow would chill us from the inside, and we knew that was dangerous.

At one point we heard a raven calling above us. We watched as it landed on a snowbank about a hundred yards in front of us along the trail of the moose. When we were halfway to the raven, it started sliding down a snowbank on its back. As soon as it got to the bottom, the raven would walk back to the top, then repeat the stunt. "I can't believe it," I said.

"Ravens do that kind of stuff," Raymond said.

"He's a real clown."

"That's what the stories say. He's lazy, too, and a thief—hardly ever gets his own food. He fools everybody, so he gets by easy."

"But Johnny was named after him."

"Named after Raven's eye, that's what he said in the letter. Raven's Eye is a good name for a hunter, don't you think? Raven knows the land better than anyone; the old stories say he made it in the first place. Ravens see everything—they know everything that's going on, what's going to happen."

As we approached the snowbank, the raven flew away, croaking.

"He never had to tell us about the moose," Raymond

said. "He didn't need us. He'd get fed anyway when the wolves took the moose down. But everybody knows stories about ravens helping people when they feel like it."

The amount of blood on the moose trail seemed to stay the same. It seemed that when the wolves had first attacked, on the Yukon side, they hadn't inflicted a serious injury. The moose was still strong, Raymond said, but the wolves were patient. He said that the wolves were driving the moose down off the mountains and into the bottom of Deadmen Valley on purpose. There would be places down in the bottom of the valley where they could use the deep snow to their advantage.

Raymond was right: the trail kept leading to Deadmen Valley. From a ridge, we spotted the wolves the third day. In the distance the moose was crossing a clearing with seven or eight wolves trotting behind. We kept going, slowing down as we encountered deeper snow in the valley. The trail showed the moose sinking through all the way to the ground—four feet or so. We didn't know how close we really were, but then we heard the moose up ahead moaning in agony. The trail was showing more blood. The wolves had attacked again.

Raymond carried his rifle at the ready. We both knew this moose was our last chance. With its meat we could wait out the rest of the winter. We shoed faster as a light snow began to fall. Half an hour later the daylight was going down. From the moaning of the moose, we knew we were close, and we walked much more cautiously. The size of the wolves' tracks astonished me— five inches across in the fresh snow.

We caught sight of them again in a clearing up ahead where the moose had foundered in deep snow, then

162

turned to face them. It was a cow moose. Without antlers, she had only her front hooves for defense. They made formidable weapons as she turned to fend off the wolves darting in on her backside. Through the falling snow I counted seven of them: two yellowish white, two gray, and three black, much bigger than I would have thought possible.

We crept to the edge of the trees. The moose was no more than a hundred yards away, encircled by the wolves. The moose looked ghostly in the dim light with the snow accumulating on her back. "Maybe we should wait until tomorrow," I whispered to Raymond.

"They'll finish her tonight," he whispered back. "It's got to be now."

"Can you get closer, go out into the clearing?"

"They'll spook. I don't want them to get into the woods."

Raymond got out of his snowshoes. Then he knelt down, laid the rifle across the sled load, took off his mask and his gloves, and braced himself. He took forever with his aim. When the shot went off, it sounded unbelievably loud in the cold, dense air. The wolves darted away and the moose did, too, stopping after a short distance, looking around. "Missed," Raymond whispered.

He ejected the shell and brought the last bullet into the chamber, fastened the bolt down. "She's dragging something behind her," I said, pointing to what looked like thick rope.

"Her intestines," Raymond said. "The wolves already opened her up."

The wolves, hanging back at the edge of the trees, were fully aware of us now.

"Got to try again," Raymond said. "There's nothing else to do, not now."

Raymond took aim. I held my breath. The rifle thundered.

Nothing. The moose just stood there, unmoving.

I closed my eyes, swaying on weary legs, trying to accept what had happened. It was over for us now.

When I looked again, I saw the moose turn and trot toward the trees. Then she stopped and looked around.

Suddenly the moose collapsed, crashing to the snow.

"What—what happened?" I stammered at Raymond.

Raymond was still staring at the moose. The amazement on his face was turning to understanding. "I must have shot her in the heart," he said. "That's what happens when you get 'em right in the heart."

A raven showed up within minutes, then two, three, four others. Raymond turned to the business of skinning and butchering. I got busy with the ax, starting a fire at the edge of the trees and building a lean-to under a sheltering spruce. The ravens ate gluttonously from the entrails and the organs, flying off just before dark. I heaped dead branches onto the fire and lit up the whole area. I hadn't noticed the wolves since they'd scattered, but now, back in the trees, their eyes reflected the firelight.

Raymond chose the tongue first, and this time I tried it, too, in memory of Johnny. Fat from our steaks, roasting on sticks, was sizzling and dripping into the fire. We ate our fill. When we were done, we covered all the meat with snow to keep down the scent, then piled heavy branches on top of that.

"Do we still want to build the brush teepee right here by the moose?" I asked, looking into the darkness for the eyes of the wolves but not seeing them.

"We've got to protect this meat," Raymond said. "That comes first. We'll have to build a cache, get all this meat up high where animals can't get it."

"We already have a cache at the cabin," I pointed out. "How far could the cabin be?"

"It's at the other end of the valley, maybe fifteen kilometers. . . . That would be a long way to pull that meat on the toboggan, that's for sure, and it would take more than one load."

I let out a whoop. "Think how warm we'd be back in the cabin for the rest of the winter! Man, that would be Fat City."

From that moment we could think of nothing but how to get ourselves back into the cabin. We'd have to split up, we decided. One of us would pull half the meat to the cabin while the other stayed to protect the rest. Without question, we needed every bit of the meat to carry us through until breakup in May.

"I'll make the first run," I said. "Got to keep in training, since I'm not playing football this year."

I could see he was going to let me have it. Through unbroken snow the first run was going to be brutal, and I had more brute strength.

"You take the fire starter," Raymond said. "I can keep the fire going here without it."

"We only have one ax. . . . You need it, and I need it."

"I've got the bow saw to make firewood. Everyone says wolves don't attack people, but in case they do while you're hauling all that meat, you better have that ax along."

In the morning we wrapped half the meat in the blue tarp and secured it on the toboggan, then tied the camp gear I would need on top of that. Raymond wouldn't let me go without squeezing Johnny's moccasins into the packsack on my back. Then he hung the fire starter from my neck and said, "See you later, buddy."

I started to pull, and he added, "Watch out for overflow. And don't keep going if no animals are moving in the woods. If it gets that cold, stop and make camp!"

"You keep that fire burning," I called over my shoulder.

It was as bad as we guessed it would be, pulling that toboggan, but it could be done. Slow and steady, I kept telling myself. Just keep leaning into that pull rope. Grab a root and dig, as my father always liked to say. Every step you're one step closer.

By midday the mercury was down in the bulb—sixty degrees below zero, as low as the thermometer could read. I could feel the cold air sinking down out of the mountains and spreading out on the valley floor, feeling very much like a substance though it couldn't be seen. Was this the cold Raymond had predicted from the coppery sun?

How cold was it getting? I wondered. Was it even colder than sixty below? Should I turn back? I looked behind me and saw a trail of fog that my breath had made. Give up what I'd accomplished getting this far? The sooner we could move back into the cabin the better. I was thinking with my legs instead of my brain.

I was wearing almost everything I had, including the face mask. With the cap pulled over the mask and the stiff hair of the parka ruff ringing my face, I knew I didn't have a chance of hearing wolves sneaking up on me, so I kept looking back and all around. I never saw them. I trudged forward, using the bald mountain for my reference point. For a brief time the sun rose above it. Twice I needed to leave the toboggan and climb high enough to catch a glimpse of the gates of the canyon on the downstream end of the Nahanni's run through Deadmen Valley. That's where the cabin sat. Six or seven miles to go.

In the afternoon twilight the cold deepened. The trees were freezing and splitting, and the streambeds made an eerie drumming *spaaaaaang* that resounded away under the ice. With the weight I was pulling, I was making such poor time I was reluctant to think about quitting with the daylight. I remembered that I should be looking around to see if animals were still moving in the woods. I hadn't seen any squirrels that I could recall, or rabbits, or fresh tracks of any kind. But then, I told myself, I hadn't been looking.

If I did stop, I would face all the struggle of making camp. No, I was doing okay. . . . I was going so slow, I should put in another hour or two. That way I wouldn't have to spend two nights out before I got to the cabin. When the twilight was gone I kept pulling by the surreal blazing-cold white light of the full moon, in and out of the long timber shadows. Far off, two owls were talking across the frozen stillness. The way sound carried in the cold, I wondered how far apart they might be.

I just kept going. Though I didn't realize it, I was half-frozen, too cold to think. If I just kept moving, I told myself, I'd stay warm, warm enough. At one point I came off a ridge and began to cross a stream bottom. The air was so cold down there it felt as if I was wading in cold water even if I wasn't. But in another couple of seconds I realized that's exactly what I *was* doing. My snowshoes sank suddenly into knee-deep slush hidden beneath the snow.

The pain struck instantly in my legs. My mind came

suddenly awake. I was in serious, serious trouble. I waded out of the overflow, the snowshoes icing before my eyes. I jerked the toboggan around and pulled for the nearest cluster of spruce. My feet were numb already. With frozen feet, I knew I'd be dead; it would be only a matter of time. I dropped my mitts and tried to undo the frozen bindings around my boots, but I was getting nowhere with my gloves on, losing way too much time. I pulled my gloves off and tore at the icy bindings with my bare fingers.

Once I was out of my snowshoes I reached for the ax on the toboggan. I turned to the trees, slashing the dead lower limbs fast as I could. I should have thought to put my gloves back on. But I wasn't thinking. I only knew I couldn't lose any time.

I gathered kindling, raced back to the toboggan for birchbark. My hands were freezing fast. I pulled dry socks and Johnny's moccasins from the packsack, and then I tried to pull the fire starter free from inside my parka and under my shirt.

My fingers wouldn't work. I had to hook my thumb under the cord and work it up and around my head.

I managed to pull the fire starter into its two halves. The white cube of fuel fell to the ground. At first I thought I'd lost it in the snow. Then I tried to pick it up.

I couldn't.

Now I realized that my fingers weren't going to be able to open my pocketknife so I could rough up the surface of the cube. I've killed myself, I thought.

Do something quick!

I picked up the cube the only way I could, with my teeth, and then I knelt low over the birchbark. I chewed up the cube with my face right down to the birchbark, letting the little pieces drop in as small an area as I could keep them.

With hands like clubs, I managed to grip the two halves of the fire starter between my thumbs and palms, and I showered sparks on my tinder again and again.

Finally a piece of the white stuff caught. It flamed up faithfully, and I got some birchbark over the flame. The birchbark burned hot and spread the flames. My kindling caught, and so did my small wood. I tried to warm up my hands, then realized I'd just burned my right palm. I pulled my hands away and warmed them up just enough to make them work again, then went to tearing at the laces of my boots.

With two pairs of dry socks and Johnny's moccasins on my feet, and my hands back in my gloves, I grabbed up the ax and went back to slashing branches to revive the fire, which had almost gone out. Then I noticed a small standing dead spruce in the moonlight. I ran to it and shattered it with a few blows. I whacked it in two and dragged both pieces over the fire. The flames began to climb up through the branches.

I could feel my feet again. They were nipped but not really frostbit. I knew I'd come within a few minutes of having both of them turn to dead flesh.

The night was just getting colder. But there was wood here, enough wood to keep a blazing fire going through the night. If there hadn't been all this wood, this close to where I'd gotten my feet wet . . .

I had all the hours of the night to feed that fire and think about my mistakes. To remember my father's warnings and Raymond's, to think about how stupid I'd been. The fire burned a well in the snow down to the ground. I stayed as close to the fire as I could, with the

170

cold always attacking at my back. I boiled water from melted snow. After I'd drunk my fill, I boiled another half pot, and out of curiosity tossed the boiling water into the air. It made a great *whoosh* and turned into fog before it ever hit the ground. I tended to the burn on my hand. I counted myself extremely lucky to be alive.

Never sleeping, I waited out the night, then pulled hard all the next day. The cabin made a beautiful sight as I hauled in at last. I fetched our ladder and shouldered all the meat up into the cache. I ate well and spent the night inside. The cabin still smelled of wolverine, but on the present scale of things that didn't even constitute an annoyance. I kept thinking about Raymond, picturing him out there in this cold. I worried about his fire and I worried about the wolves.

The extreme cold showed no sign of letting up. In the morning there was a quarter inch of frost on every nailhead on the inside of the cabin door. I knew Raymond wouldn't want me to try to travel in these conditions. I waited one day, but the mercury never climbed out of the well in the bottom of the bulb. I knew I couldn't wait any longer to get back to him. Before light the following day, I was on my way.

With my own trail to follow through broken snow and only the camp gear on the toboggan, I made it all the way back to Raymond in one long haul. When at last I spotted his campfire, I gave a shout, and he hollered back. After four days of pure silence, the sound of his voice brought tears to my eyes.

Raymond was indeed happy to see me. "I was afraid something happened to you," he said. "Did you keep going in that cold, or what?"

I had to confess about the overflow and about everything that had happened. Seeing his face as I told it, I scared myself all over again. "That's twice," he said. "You're pretty lucky, but I think you better stay away from water from now on."

Raymond had made a delicious thick soup from the head meat of the moose with plenty of fat thrown in. We were going to take the liver and kidneys along with the second load of meat, anything that could conceivably be eaten. What was left of the heart he gave to the ravens.

We waited a couple of days, until it warmed up to forty below. I undid the bandaging on the palm of my right hand, and we took a look. It ached all the time, especially at night when I had to lie down and wasn't doing anything. "It looks like raw meat," Raymond observed. I cleaned it with warm water, put some antiseptic salve on it, and rewrapped it with fresh gauze. "At least it's not getting infected," I said. "Maybe it's too cold to get infected."

This time we could trade off pulling the toboggan. Though the trail was twice broken now, the weight made us earn every yard. Raymond wondered how I'd done it the first time, and so did I.

We approached the cabin at noon the next day, the last day of January. We knew we could get by now for the rest of the winter. I said, "'We're going to make it now. We're home free." That was about a minute before we found two of the legs of our food cache broken off and the cache itself toppled on the ground. All the meat I'd cached from the first trip was gone. Everywhere we looked we saw the tracks of an enormous bear.

19

Winter bear," Raymond said, his voice hushed and awed. The length and the width of the tracks had my heart beating like thunder. My first thought was that we had no shells left for the rifle. I looked between the trees expecting at any moment to see the monster that made the tracks. "What's a winter bear?" I whispered. "Polar bear?"

"Grizzly," he said quietly, looking over his shoulder. "Probably a big male, from the size of these prints."

"But why isn't it hibernating?"

"It didn't put on enough fat to hibernate. Maybe there was a bad berry crop, or its teeth are too worn down."

In frustration, I kicked at one of the cache's broken stilts. Like the other two legs, they had originally been living trees sawed off to support the cache. They'd looked sound from the outside, but inside they were rotten. Raymond dropped his outer mitts, then went around the toboggan undoing our slipknots. All the while he was glancing over his shoulder, which struck even more terror in my heart. "We better hurry," he said. "Get our things into the cabin and figure out what to do with this meat. Bears can smell like anything. It could come back."

We threw our things inside the cabin, plus the last of the firewood—enough to get us by when night fell. All the while we were looking over our shoulders. "Keep watching," Raymond warned. "Bears move quiet. You probably won't hear it coming."

Now we turned to the meat on the toboggan. How to protect it now that the cache was down on the ground? "On the top of the cabin?" I wondered.

"Not high enough. The roof might cave in if the bear gets up on there."

"Hang pieces of it from tree branches?"

"Ravens and camprobbers would get it."

I stood there stamping my feet and smacking my mitts together. There was nothing left between my ears but ice. Then Raymond thought of the solution: put the toboggan up in a tree, across a couple of branches. Tie it down, repack it, cover it with the tarp and branches so the birds couldn't get at it.

Easier said than done at fifty degrees below zero, but what choice did we have?

With only the ax for protection, we went to get the ladder, upright in a tight cluster of spruces where I'd left it. Then we scouted all around the cabin in widening circles, searching for the right tree. Finally we found one barely back from the bank of the Nahanni, across from the stretch of water that even now remained open. It was a giant spruce standing all by itself several hundred yards from the protection of the cabin. Our ladder reached its lowest limbs at about the thirteen-foot level. At that point two substantial branches poked out from the trunk about five feet apart—just what we needed to support the toboggan.

Back at the cabin Raymond said we should pack both

174

army boxes with meat before we sledded the rest to our new cache. "Just in case," he said.

"You've got a head on your shoulders," I told him. "Mine froze off a couple of days ago."

"So let's get going while mine's still attached!"

I couldn't help laughing at our insanely desperate situation. "Welcome back to the valley of headless men, eh?"

With the ax we hacked the meat into shapes we could cram into the army boxes, then fastened the lids down and left the boxes outside the cabin door. After that we sledded the toboggan to the tree, looking all around for the bear in the twilight. It was impossible to shake the sensation that we were being watched. "Whatever you do," Raymond whispered, "don't turn your back on one of those bears. Don't run, or it'll chase you. Talk to it."

"Talk to it?"

"Talk to it nice. Let it know what you are. Don't look it in the eye, don't get it mad. Is the ax handy? It's all we've got."

Suddenly I felt sick through and through. "I left it at the cabin," I confessed. "Should I go get it?"

"Let's just get the meat up in the tree."

The canopy of the spruce's branches had shed the snow so effectively that the ground was bare below it, making for a good staging area. Raymond went up the ladder first and stood on the branch. I started working the empty toboggan up as he pulled from above. We muscled the toboggan into the tree, and Raymond worked it across the two big branches. I went halfway up and handed him the tarp. Then I went back down for the first piece of meat.

"Too late," Raymond whispered.

"What do you mean?"

"Look out on the river."

I couldn't see anything. "Quit joking," I said.

"It's coming toward us."

I still couldn't see anything.

"Get up here!"

Now I could see the bear, huge and silver, soundlessly crossing the river ice, more like a ghost bear than a flesh-and-blood creature. I recognized the big hump over the shoulders, yet this apparition looked nothing like my conception of a grizzly. This bear looked as if it had been carved from crystal. Then I realized that its fur was entirely armored in ice, giving it this ghostlike appearance. The bear had gotten into open water and now its fur was draped with hundreds of daggers of ice. My heart was in my throat as it paused, lifting its nose, taking the scent of the frozen moose meat and maybe of me.

"Get up here!"

I grabbed a piece of moose meat and climbed up the ladder. I handed the meat to Raymond, then joined him on the branch. When I turned around to look, the bear rose over the top of the riverbank, paused to sniff the air again, and kept coming. "Holy cow," I muttered.

Halfway to the tree the bear stood on two legs and woofed several times, looking all around. I had serious doubts, trying to gauge the standing height of the bear, about our safety on this limb. I looked up into the tree; we could scramble to higher branches if we had to. For a moment the bear went down on all fours, then back on hind legs again, roaring a challenge that could have

176

knocked trees down. "He smells us," Raymond whispered.

Now the bear came on cautiously to the meat and hung its head low, growling like a dog over a bone. We could see every icicle clinging to its fur. I thought the bear might not be aware of us after all, but suddenly it swung away from the meat, stood on two hind legs again, and looked right up at us, roaring horribly.

We tried to pull up the ladder, but we couldn't budge it from where we were crouching. "Should I knock it over?" I asked.

"We need it to get down. He can't come up it anyway. He's too heavy."

We looked back down only to see the bear, all glistening with ice, moving closer yet. Then the bear stood to its full height against the ladder, just below us, and began to climb it. I rose, reaching for the next limb above me. When a couple of rungs broke beneath its weight, the bear stood up and began to throw its weight against the ladder with a rocking motion, roaring with frustration. Its breath made fog that blasted over us, warm and smelling of the inside of its gut.

With a loud crack, the ladder broke completely in half.

The bear turned back to our precious moose meat, gnawing on it while keeping up a continuous growl.

"Don't worry about us," I called to the bear. "We aren't going anywhere."

The winter bear growled louder. "Don't get him mad," Raymond whispered.

"We're going to freeze up if we can't move around," I said.

"I know."

There was nothing to be done. All we could do was rearrange ourselves a little so we could sit on the toboggan, and then it was a matter of waiting the bear out. Early on we thought the bear might be leaving, when it took a huge hunk of meat in its mouth and ghosted away, but we could still hear it growling somewhere out there. It was back again within five minutes.

When the bear had carried away the last of the meat, we were still pinned in the tree with the cold seeping through every layer and into our bones. It got dark, and the moon appeared over the mountains, just past full. The growling went on and on, wherever the bear was, not that far away. "How are your feet?" I asked. "Like concrete," Raymond answered.

"Same here. Man, we're going to freeze solid. When they find us, they're going to wonder what we were doing up here."

No reply from Raymond. I thought I better keep talking at least. I said, "Think about being too hot."

"Impossible," he said.

"When my dad and I were at Big Bend out in west Texas, it got to 118 degrees."

"How hot is that?"

"Even lizards burn their feet on it."

"I've never seen a lizard, except in a book."

"Most of them can't tolerate the sand during the daytime in the middle of the summer. They stay hidden underground, or in shady cracks in the rocks. But there's this one kind of lizard I saw tearing across a sand dune—whenever it stopped moving, it lifted its front left leg and its back right leg at the same time, and balanced on the other two. After a few seconds the feet on the sand got too hot, so it traded off with the other two, back and forth, back and forth. It looked goofy, but I guess it works.''

"They got turtles in Texas? I never saw one of those either.''

"All kinds of turtles, including snapping turtles. They sit on the bottom of the river, open their jaws, and wag their tongue back and forth for a fishing lure. Ever heard of an armadillo?''

"Is it a kind of turtle?''

"Not a turtle. I don't know what they are, really. Maybe a kind of anteater with armor.''

"For real?''

"Sure they're real. They look like a little armored car, but they've got feet instead.''

He started chuckling, then giggling. Then he shifted his position. "Man, I'm cold.''

"I can still hear 'keep out of its way.' I don't trust him any farther than I can throw him.''

Raymond laughed. "I never heard that expression. Or 'Holy cow' either.''

"You don't watch enough TV.''

"I thought you said I watch too much. You really don't watch TV? Or just fooling?''

"Not much.''

"How come?''

"Oh, because of my mother, I guess. She liked to read, I really remember that. I've been thinking about her a lot lately.''

"Yeah," he said quietly. "I know what you mean. I keep thinking about Johnny, stuff I learned from him.''

"Well, now you have that bush education that he said you should get.''

179

"That's for sure. . . . But it doesn't look like I'm going to graduate."

There was nothing I could say, nothing honest. Instead I said, "I don't hear the bear anymore."

"He could still be close by."

"I know."

"Should we take a chance?"

"We have to, or we'll freeze to death."

The trunk of the tree was much too big around for us to try shinnying down it. We were going to have to hang from a limb and then drop to the ground.

I got up. I was stiff as stone. If I dropped to the ground and the bear rushed me, then what?

I shucked my mitts, crouched, and got ready to lower myself, using the limb. My gloved hands weren't going to be much use: they were too cold to really grip with. I encircled the branch with my forearms, then lowered my weight over the side as slowly as I could. I was so frozen up, I couldn't really hang on and then time my drop. I broke loose before I was ready and fell heavily to the frozen ground, tumbling quick as I could to take the weight from my feet. I knew right away I'd hurt my knee.

"You okay?" Raymond whispered.

"I hurt my knee—sprained it maybe. I don't know if you should try . . . the ground's hard as steel."

"I can't stay up here. I gotta try it."

"See if you can tuck and roll as you hit the ground."

Raymond lost his grip before he was ready to drop, just sort of fell off the branch. He tried to right himself in midair but came down hard on his right foot, which buckled. Even through his red mask I could see him react to the pain.

180

"I hurt it," he whispered apologetically. "I think I hurt it bad."

I waited a minute, looking for the bear, expecting to see its dim shape in the starlight. "Can you walk?"

"Don't think so," he managed to say.

"I'm going to lift you up now. Put all your weight on your good leg. Use my shoulder."

I had him standing up on one leg. He said, "What about your knee?"

"Don't worry about it. Ready?"

"Ready," he said. "Let's go."

At last the fire in the stove was backing off the deep cold that had settled inside the cabin. With the stove door cracked, I could see to unlace Raymond's boots. His face in the flickering light of the fire was contorted with pain. "Sprains can hurt really bad," I said. "Let's hope it's only a sprain." He flinched and sucked in his breath as I eased the boot around his heel.

In the first-aid kit we had two kinds of pain medicine: a bottle of aspirin we'd almost used up and another smaller prescription bottle we hadn't touched yet. The smaller one read: *Take one to two tablets by mouth every three hours as needed for pain.* In handwriting underneath was written: *For major pain. Do not use with head injuries.* When I read that part to Raymond he managed a grin and said, "I guess I was lucky I hurt my foot."

Both our water bottles were dry. He stuck one pill at a time way down his throat and swallowed them. I said I'd go get some water after I wrapped his foot.

He grimaced, shook his head.

"Don't wrap your foot?"

"Don't get water," he said between his teeth.

"Why not?"

He put both his hands up in the air, spreading his fingers like huge claws, then raked me on the arm.

"Oh, I forgot," I said. "Probably we shouldn't bring the boxes of meat inside the cabin, either."

He nodded vigorously.

"But I'll string them up in a tree first thing in the morning."

"Good. But what if he breaks the rope or chews it? Bears are smart."

"Let me think. . . . That cable from the airplane isn't very far away, the one Johnny used for the snare. I'll use that for the part he can reach."

As I pulled off Raymond's socks, I said, "You might be out of next week's game, but we'll have you back in the lineup the week after."

The foot looked bad—bruised and swelling fast. I said, "In my professional opinion . . . a bad sprain."

"Hope so."

"You'll see," I said, even though I wasn't at all sure. "Tell me where it hurts the most."

"My whole ankle."

I began to wrap his ankle in a figure eight with an elastic bandage. I made it secure enough for support but not tight enough to cut off circulation. "Now we should ice it," I said.

"No way. It still feels freezing cold."

"Just don't get it anywhere near the fire then." Gently as I could, I worked two pairs of wool socks back over his foot. Then I helped him into his sleeping bag and stuffed some clothes under his leg to elevate it a little. "I'll get some fresh spruce bedding in here tomorrow," I said. "Lot of tips—this stuff is awful rough."

"What about your knee?" he asked. "You're limping around yourself. Take some of those pills."

"It's okay," I told him. "We're both messed up, but you're more messed up than I am."

Lucky for Raymond, he slept after a while. I sat up stoking the fire, ax within reach and listening for the bear, which I kept thinking I was hearing moving around outside. I was keenly aware of my thirst and hunger, and our deadly situation. The winter bear willing, I could reach our boxes of meat, I could fetch water. I could keep us warm, but I couldn't supply what we needed most: hope. No hope now of making it until May.

At first light I laced up the snowshoes and went looking for the wire cable from the airplane. It was farther away than I remembered, and I took a couple of hours finding it, limping around in the trees and imagining at every moment the approach of the bear. I was even more scared than I'd been in the actual presence of the bear. Raymond had been with me then, and that made all the difference.

Back at the cabin, Raymond was no better but awfully glad to see me. I crept to the creek for water. Every nerve in my body was screaming false alarms. After that I strung the army boxes in the trees, always with an eye over my shoulder. I had to cook out in front of the cabin on an open fire—that way we wouldn't be inviting the bear inside with the smell of meat. And if the bear came around, it might be deterred by the fire. I helped Raymond get around so he wouldn't fall and make his injury worse.

Raymond sat at the table to eat. We put away two huge moose steaks with thick trimmings of fat. All the same, we agreed that with only the two boxes of moose meat, we had to go back to eating only once a day. We didn't talk about how there wasn't enough to pull us through, even if we cut back to starvation rations. We both knew that.

I could tell Raymond's foot felt just as bad or worse. He kept taking his pills. We were going to go by my watch so he wouldn't run out of them any sooner than he had to. My knee was going to come around if I just didn't work it too hard. I was pretty sure by now it wasn't anything really bad.

The sky was extraordinarily orange all above the bald mountain in advance of the sunrise. Raymond said we'd probably have snow coming. I had to go out on the snowshoes and find firewood. There weren't any more dead trees within ten minutes of the cabin. The bear was everywhere and nowhere. I kept imagining its silver shape and soundless approach between the trees.

The sun rose at ten forty-five in the morning. At least I could count on the February daylight helping out a little bit more each day. I spent the rest of the day felling dead trees, hauling logs back to the cabin, hoping Raymond's foot would improve soon. I was thinking furiously about escape. I saw no way out but trying our luck down the Nahanni once again. In the evening I told Raymond I thought we were going to have to try it, and he thought so too. "Think how long we've had this vicious cold spell," I said. "In another week, the open spots in the river are even more likely to have frozen up. And you'll be ready to go."

Raymond just nodded his head. He didn't seem too

convinced. We both knew that the patch of water just up the river from the cabin remained as open as ever.

The next day I hauled logs to the cabin again, and in the afternoon I began to saw and split more firewood. My palm kept cracking open along the creases, but that couldn't be helped. Then I broke the last saw blade.

For a second I just stared at the broken blade. Then I threw the useless saw down on the ground, kicked it, and felt a bolt of pain course through my knee. I looked up to see Raymond at the cabin door, standing on one foot and watching me. "It's okay, Gabe," he said. "That last blade was bound to go sometime. We can get by with the ax. Hey, look at the clouds. It's warming up—might snow."

Raymond went back inside. I thought of covering the firewood with the tarp, then remembered that the tarp was still with the toboggan up in the spruce where the bear had treed us. I needed to fetch the toboggan, too; we were going to need it for our gear when we made our break. And there was a hunk of moose meat rolled up in the tarp.

I cut a couple of slender birches and dragged them over to our busted ladder beneath the big spruce, the ax under my arm and my head swiveling around, looking for the bear. I splinted the ladder poles with the birches, the quickest makeshift repair I could manage, and I climbed into the tree. Carefully I lowered the toboggan to the ground and then came down with the piece of meat.

I wasn't really on guard as I made my beeline to the cabin. I thought I was home safe; my eye was on the door and I was thinking about Raymond. I was only fifty feet from the cabin when I heard that ominous, unmistakable woof, once, twice. There was the winter bear, right there, standing under the suspended metal boxes no farther from me than I was from the cabin. The ghostlike bear, all too real, came down to all fours with a roar in its throat, laying its ears back and fixing its small dark eyes on me. Its jaws were making an awful snapping and clicking sound.

I wanted to turn and bolt for the cabin. "Don't run," I remembered Raymond saying. "Don't turn your back on him." I shucked my mitts and held tight to the ax with both hands. I remembered I had the piece of meat on the toboggan right behind me. "Talk nice," I remembered. But I never had a chance to talk. Fast as a train, the bear charged. I got set to try to do him some damage.

No more than fifteen feet from me, the bear came to an abrupt halt and stood up roaring, a mountain of ice and claws and teeth. I held out the ax toward the bear, without quite looking him in the eye, and spoke as calmly as I could manage: "We keep this ax real sharp, winter bear. If you try to hurt me, I'm going to floss your teeth."

The bear glanced toward the cabin. I heard Raymond's voice over there say something in Slavey and then add "Go away" in English.

The bear went down on all fours, eyeing me, then Raymond. Its nose was twitching; I realized he smelled the meat. I backed up a couple of steps, bent down slowly, then tossed the meat in its direction. The grizzly took the meat, then retreated twenty feet or so. It stood once more, with the meat in its mouth, then loped into the trees with a shuffling gait, its head held close to the ground.

My knees were so weak I could barely make it to the cabin. "Floss his teeth?" Raymond said as I reached the door.

"I didn't know what to say!"

"You sounded like you meant it." Raymond hopped back inside, taking a seat at the table. "You did everything right."

"I was all jelly! What did *you* say? If you hadn't distracted him . . . Did you say something in Slavey?"

"I called him 'friend.' "

"How come you said it in Slavey?"

"I didn't think about it. . . . I guess because I figured he would understand Slavey."

I busted out laughing. "That sort of makes sense. Sorry I had to feed him."

"I think that was a pretty good idea."

"Will he come back?"

"I don't know. Keep watching out for him. A bear in that condition might stalk a human being."

My heart was still hammering like thunder. "What if he comes through the door?"

"There's nothing we could really block the door with if that bear wanted to come in."

An hour later, just as it was getting dark, I got up enough courage to peek outside. It was starting to snow in stinging, miniature crystals. I covered my stack of wood outside with the tarp and leaned the toboggan up against the back of the stack. Then I brought in as much wood as we could keep inside the cabin. I stacked quite a bit of it against the door. "I'll have to rearrange it to go back outside," I said to Raymond, "but as my dad always says, 'What's time to a hog?' "

"I don't get what that means," Raymond said.

"It makes more sense than a lot of his jokes. Try this one: 'What's the difference between a duck?' "

" 'Between a duck'?" Raymond repeated. "I don't get it."

"Neither do I. Are you ready for the answer?"

"I'm ready."

I smiled, just like my father always did when he told this, and said, "The other leg is the same."

Raymond still looked confused. I said, "Don't bust a gut trying to figure it out. I've been working on it for about ten years. How's your foot?"

"Maybe a little better." I couldn't tell if he believed it or not. Maybe the pain medicine was helping him to believe it, but he was going to run out of the pills soon.

"Your hair's getting long and shaggy," I told him.

"So is yours. You got a beard now, too."

I stroked what was left of my face after all the wind and cold and that woolen mask. "Feels like a poor excuse for a beard. Glad we don't have a mirror along—we'd scare ourselves to death."

"I got a scar here on my forehead?"

"It looks great—gives you even more character. We won't cut our hair—we'll be rock-and-roll stars."

He was amused, but he said to me thoughtfully, "I want to get another guitar. Maybe learn fiddle, too. Some of those old guys could teach me fiddle."

Raymond asked me to bring down one of the remaining beaver pelts that Johnny had stretched with willow frames and hung up on the wall. Then he took the sheath knife off his belt and started carefully scraping the fur from the hide. "I want to try to fix up Johnny's drum," he explained. "Make a new drumskin for it."

"Sounds like a good idea," I said. "That wolverine really made a mess of it."

I kept watching the weather. It warmed all the way up to zero and just kept snowing. Now the snow had some moisture in it; it was quite a bit heavier. I fretted about the new snow making it harder to pull the toboggan when we were ready to leave, but there was nothing to be done. We just had to wait for Raymond's foot to heal. I wished I had a book to read. It would take my mind off the waiting and also off thinking about what was going to happen to us. Then I got an idea. Actually, watching Raymond work on that drum made me think of it. I could try to make a model of a log house, just like the one my father and I were going to build down in the hill country. I got really excited just thinking about it.

Over the next four days, every time I went out with the ax to go chop ice at the creek and haul water, I also brought back alder branches. Smooth and straight and strong, with thin dark bark, they made perfect model logs. I laid out the base of the log house just a few inches in from the edges of the table. This was going to be a sizable model. Knowing my dad, he wouldn't settle for a simple rectangle. And he'd want it to be huge, two stories high where you walked in the front door. He'd mentioned a special room for a pool table— I wasn't going to leave that out.

I enjoyed notching all the little logs, making the door and window openings, thinking about how I was going to do the roof. I let my mind drift, and it shortly drifted from sentimental to morbid. I was thinking that if I did end up dead, at least my dad would get to find this log house I made for him. He'd come here after somebody

190

found us, they'd figure out we'd been staying at this cabin, he'd know I'd been thinking about him. . . .

After studying the construction of Johnny's hand drum, Raymond had removed the torn drumskin and fitted his new one over Johnny's birch frame. He reworked the fine spruce roots in a perfect imitation of Johnny's lashing where it ran through the birch frame and crisscrossed on the underside of the drum.

We would work silently for a long while, and then we'd get to talking. Our conversations went on far into the night. Raymond had much more curiosity than I'd ever realized about what life was like down in the States, or "the South," as he called it. At first I thought he was talking about Mississippi, Alabama, Louisiana and so on, but then I realized that everything south of the Northwest Territories was "the South" to him. He was trying to picture how big San Antonio was, and I told him it had more than a million people. He kept trying to picture all those houses, all those people, all those cars and freeways. "I don't think I'd want to live there," he said. "Too many people. What we got up in the North is lots of land."

I told him about the piece of land close to my grandparents' place, how it used to be covered with hundreds of live oak trees, and how I would always climb into this one certain tree and hang out there. I told him that when they built a big shopping mall on that land, they didn't even save one tree when they made the parking lot.

"How come?" he said.

"Because it was too much trouble, I guess, and would've added cost. To find open land, you have to go farther and farther away."

He was trying to picture it. Then he asked, "Is it true that people are always shooting each other? Like it looks like on TV?"

"It's in the news every night," I admitted.

"What about suicide?"

It seemed like a strange question. "I guess it's a big problem," I said. "I don't know much about it, really."

Then he talked about growing up in Nahanni Butte, about fixing snowmobiles, about the winter road, about the boat they would use to get back and forth to Fort Simpson in the summer when it was light all night. "What about mosquitoes?" I asked.

"They get real bad in June," he said. "But the gnats and the blackflies later are worse."

He went on to tell me all about his family: his mother and his father, his big sister, Monique, who was nineteen and lived with his grandmother, his younger brother, Alfred, who was nine, and his younger sister, Dora, who was seven. In the midst of this, to my surprise, he told me that he wanted to go back to the boarding school at Yellowknife. "I want to graduate from there," he said. "Not many kids from Nahanni ever did. I thought I could do it. I knew I was smart enough. . . . I just didn't have my mind made up strong enough."

"I'm sure you can," I said. "I know you can."

"Johnny thought it was important. Even if it's going to be hard."

I could tell there was something else he was wanting to say. "What is it?" I asked.

Raymond looked away, then said, "I had an older brother . . . he got angry a lot. He went to that school in Yellowknife. My parents say he got lost there. They

192

told me to come back if I felt like I was going to get lost.''

"Your brother doesn't come home anymore?" I wondered, all confused.

"He killed himself."

I felt like all the breath had been knocked out of me, I didn't know how to react. I tried to say something, but I couldn't find any words except "I'm sorry."

Raymond was looking down at the drum in his hands. "Don't feel sorry about it—that's what my mother says to me. She'd say, 'Don't feel sorry for him or yourself. You can't change the past. You can only change the future.' She'd say, 'Just remember, Raymond, life is the greatest gift.' I always thought that was just something she heard at church. Now I know it's the truth. It's the truest thing there is.''

Then Raymond looked up from the drum and caught my eye. "I'm not going to make it, Gabe."

He'd said it with such certainty, it scared me bad. "What are you talking about?" I shot back.

"My foot. I'll wait here for you to send somebody back. Maybe they can get a helicopter in here or something."

"You're kidding," I said, racing to think of objections. But I could see he wasn't kidding.

"It's been a week. I can't put any weight on it. It's busted up bad. You have to go by yourself."

"I'll pull you out on the toboggan."

He was shaking his head. "It's too far. It's too much to pull, with all the camp gear and everything."

"I pulled half a moose."

"Not nearly as far. What about your knee?"

"It's okay," I said, which wasn't exactly true. "How

would you get firewood and water back here by yourself? I'd have to take the fire starter. What happens when your fire goes out?''

His dark eyes were back down on the drum. ''You'd have ten times better chance if you went by yourself. We'll split up the food. You can make some more firewood before you go, and I'll make sure the fire doesn't go out. You'll make it out much faster without me. Then you can send back help.''

''What about open water?'' I asked him. ''What about that? If I fall into the river, what happens to you?''

He shrugged. ''That's the way it goes, I guess.''

''I won't even think about it,'' I said. ''You'd be waiting and nobody would ever come. Everything that's happened, we've been through it together, right? Except for that once when I was on my own, and I nearly got myself killed.''

''You won't let that happen again.''

''Listen,'' I pleaded. ''You're the best friend I'm ever going to have. That's what I'm talking about. I've just been hearing about what your mother said, how life is the greatest gift. She's right. That's why we've been trying so hard to stay alive. But friendship, that's as close to the top of the list as you can get.''

Raymond seemed surprised by the strength of my outburst, but gratified. ''Okay,'' he agreed. ''We'll see if you can pull the toboggan with me on it and everything else, too. But if you can't, I stay here.''

''I can pull you out of here, I know I can.''

''Musk-ox!'' he said with a smile.

21

Don't think about how far a hundred miles is, I told myself. Don't turn around and look at the cabin. It's probably not even out of sight yet. Don't think about the hundred miles or the snow being soft or how much your load might weigh. Don't think about how much energy you've expended to get a quarter mile. If you do, you'll make yourself crazy. You'll have to admit that Raymond has to be left behind, like he said.

Think about the note you left in the cabin for your dad, the one you signed "Going for broke." That's what you have to remember. It's everything or nothing. Give it everything you've got and a whole lot more. Pull like there's no tomorrow, but don't get stupid and make mistakes or there won't be a tomorrow. It's going to take a lot of tomorrows to make it to Nahanni Butte.

I rested, panting, taking in the looming gate of the lower canyon. "There's the starting gate," I said over my shoulder.

I looked up high, maybe a thousand feet above, where the wind was whipping the snow off the high ledges. It would have made a beautiful postcard, I thought. I would title it *The Brutal Beauty of the Nahanni*. I pointed up there and said to Raymond, "We sure ain't in Texas!"

"You talk funny," he said.

"Just layin' on the accent. . . . I was thinking how Clint promised he was going to give us 'a sightseeing tour we'd never forget.' "

"Hah!" Raymond snorted.

"He delivered!" I yelled, and I leaned into the rope, lurching the toboggan into motion. That was the hardest part.

Now just keep pulling. Don't set your sights way down into the canyon. Set a goal just a hundred yards or so ahead at a time, that's plenty. One football-field length. One football field and then the next.

The cold seared my windpipe and my lungs. My sweat was falling into my eyes and freezing the lashes shut. The packsack was so heavy, digging into my shoulders, but there wasn't room for everything on the toboggan. *So far to go!* I thought, and I'm starting out a complete wreck. My knee is gimped up, and that's a fact. I just don't want Raymond to know how bad it still is. And then there's my ribs, from when I slipped on the ice and dropped the moose meat. My side's aching again from that. My lips are split open in a couple of places, so's the palm of my hand, always there throbbing to remind me. My fingers are a mess, burned in spots, chapped, cracked. Somewhere along the line frostbite got the tip of my nose and my chin. . . .

Can't do that! I told myself angrily. You wouldn't do it before; don't give in to it now. Think about somebody else—think about Raymond. Is he cold? Yes, he's cold. Will he get frostbit not moving around? I hope not—he's wearing your boots, they're warmer than his. He's wearing enough clothes to start a surplus store; he'll be okay. Johnny's parka is over him for a blanket.

What about Raymond's foot? Think about that. Think about how bone surgeons can do amazing things, even if they have to rebreak some of the bones and fasten everything with pins before they cast it. It'll feel awful good to come out of that operation with a cast on his foot finally, and then to hear he'll get normal use of it back. Maybe Wayne Gretzky won't have to worry about him becoming a hockey star, but he'll be able to do just about anything else, whatever he wants to do.

What will he want to do?

What are *you* going to do? Head back to Texas, what do you think? Head back where it's warm as soon as you can get out of here—your grandparents will take you back in a heartbeat. Spring in San Antonio! Fiesta! Think about the Battle of the Flowers, what a parade. And the Flambeaux night parade with all the torches. Think about squeezing into a few blocks with about ten thousand people at "A Night in Old San Antonio," all those girls with flowers in their hair. . . . Think about the River Walk, taking a girl out to one of those nice restaurants along the river. . . . Think about summer. . . . Think how you could lie there on a real bed with a real mattress, with only your sheet and you wouldn't even need that. . . . Think about it being too hot to sleep, what that feels like. You'll be lying there trying to remember what the cold felt like back up here in the Northwest Territories.

Trying to remember the cold? I thought. What, are you crazy? Try to *forget*.

"You're doing good," I heard Raymond call from behind me.

I stopped in my tracks, turned around, and grinned. "I'm going a lot of places in my head," I said.

"Me too."

"Think I'll go to Bermuda next. Or Hawaii. Maybe Tahiti." I finished my bottle of water.

"Trade you bottles," Raymond said. I knew he was right, I needed to keep drinking water. I took his full one and gave him mine.

Take a deep breath, heave, lean, grunt, pull. You're rolling again. Push off with that left foot, lift the right snowshoe high, swing the left arm forward and across to keep your momentum going, nothing solid down there to push off of but push anyway, left snowshoe high, right arm across. Keep believing, I told myself. Just keep pulling.

That first open water we'd met after Christmas was all iced over now. Everything looked different. Our hopes soared, but we weren't going to talk about it.

The days are longer now, I thought. That's in our favor, too. Toward twilight I set a goal of reaching a timbered island far down the frozen river. I kept pushing, and we made it. I found a spot protected by the trees. I'd have to use the remaining light to get ready for the night. It was thirty below and dropping. A ragged night coming up. No cabin; you remember what that's like. How far had we come? Don't know. Don't worry about it.

I got busy with the ax, cut plenty of spruce bedding, layered the boughs across each other, finished up with enough tips to make the endless night-torture tolerable. Then I helped Raymond out of the toboggan. He didn't think he should lie down right away, and I knew he was right. I cut him a stick to lean on and encouraged him to hop around a little, get his circulation going. Then I grabbed a snowshoe to dig a fire pit in the snow, slashed dead branches for kindling, found my birchbark, coaxed a flame into fire, and nursed it into the living force that would keep us alive through the night.

I caught my breath, warmed my hands. Then I took down three small dead spruces and dragged them over. Raymond wanted to help, so I had him start melting some snow.

I kept the fire blazing, scooped more snow into the pot, built a lean-to, then talked Raymond into lying down. He kept trying to help, but I was afraid he'd fall, and that would make things worse. I could see how tough this was going to be on Raymond, not being able to do hardly anything. I started some water to boil meat, drank some of the hot water I'd already made, and took some to him.

"You're like a house burning down," Raymond said. "Where'd you learn all this stuff?"

"Texas hill country. In Texas it gets a *lot* colder than here, and the canyons are a lot deeper."

"And there's little animals that look like armored cars?"

"Exactly. In the winter they just roll themselves up in a ball and freeze solid. What'll it be for dinner tonight?"

He flashed his bright smile. "How 'bout some moose?"

"Good selection. Specialty of the house." I took the ax and hacked out maybe a couple of pounds. After I got the meat boiling, I made some more hot water in the second pot. I knew I was already getting dehydrated and that would be a big danger, as hard as I was pulling.

At night I had to make sure to drink all the water my body could take.

With the first sign of twilight in the morning it was time to convince bone and muscle that I could even get out of the sleeping bag. The pain in my knee was still there. I needed to find more firewood, I needed to get some water going, I needed to get a little more food in my belly and Raymond's too. I needed to remember before we started out again to fill both of the water bottles full of hot water.

At last it was all done. I packed Raymond into the toboggan, laced up my snowshoes, took my place up front, stepped inside the rope. I asked Raymond if he'd ever had a dog team.

"Snowmobiles are better," he said. "Go faster too."

He could see I was playing games with my head, just stalling for time. "Don't they break down?" I asked.

"Then you fix 'em."

Once I broke the toboggan loose and started it forward, all my conversations had to take place in my head alone. Imaginary conversations, remembered conversations. Conversations with my father, conversations with Raymond, conversations with my coach back in San Antonio. My coach was trying to get me to stay. Lots of compliments. "You're hard to knock off your feet," that's what he'd said. "I like how you get the extra yards after you get hit."

I turned a bend in the canyon and saw up ahead what I'd been dreading most: a black strip of open water snaking its way down the canyon. There was an ice bridge across it, but fortunately we didn't have to try it. There was room to get around the open water on the left.

On the third day a gift came along. Just like the creeks do, the Nahanni had burst its frozen lid and spilled overflow slush for miles, melting the drifted snow that had covered the ice and refreezing it into a surface as hard and solid as an interstate highway. For a few miles we went flying around the bends in the canyon—at least that's what it felt like. I pictured it would be like this all the way down to the hot springs at the foot of the canyon. But the free ride ended when the now-frozen overflow had encountered a patch of open water. The open water was easy enough to get around, but now I was back to breaking trail through the drifts.

The following day, no more patches of open water. Maybe they were all behind us. *Pull,* you mule, you donkey, you draft horse, you dog team, you musk-ox. Think about the winter bear, the way it laid its ears back right before it charged. It can't hurt you now. Maybe it never came back because Raymond called it friend, spoke to it in Slavey. More likely it got scared off by that threat about flossing its teeth. Think about the old man finding those beaver hideouts. Now, that was slick.

Think about Johnny Raven. Remember his voice, the rivers in his face, the quills in his chin. Think how fond he became of Raymond. Think how much he wanted Raymond and you to live. Think about his hand drum, how Raymond rebuilt it, think about it right here in your packsack, going back home with Raymond. Picture your model log house, complete with tiny rock fireplace, sitting on the table back at the cabin. How your dad would love to see that model. Try to remember everything about Johnny's letter. "Take care of each other," that's what he'd said.

My heart skipped a beat when I saw that, up ahead at a bend, open water was pushing up against a cliff on the right. But we were able to pull around it once again, on the left side this time. The canyon narrowed. More open water, which was rushing out from under the ice and down to a cliff on the left side. We crossed to the right to avoid it. But the open water, after it hit the cliff on the left, angled back across the canyon, under an ice bridge, to another cliff on the right. It was the exact same situation we'd faced before.

This time the open water was only thirty feet across at the ice bridge. The bridge itself was fifteen feet wide. I stood there, imagining my body disappearing under the Nahanni ice. Eventually it would get hung up on the limbs of a tree pinned in the riverbed, or else it would just keep tumbling all the way to the Arctic Ocean.

Raymond broke the silence. "You should go across with just a packsack, with everything you'll need to make it to Nahanni Butte."

I asked him, "How come is that?"

"In case it breaks behind you. If it holds you, you can do another load and so on, until it's just me on the toboggan without any gear. That way we won't have any more weight on the bridge than we have to."

"And if I don't make it across . . . ," I said. "If I fall in, like last time . . ."

"I guess I can't pull you out. Anyway, we can't turn around and go back this time."

"So if I make it across, but the ice breaks behind me, or if I don't make it and I end up in the river, in either case you're sitting here in the toboggan—and then what?''

"Out of luck, I guess."

I thought for a second, but I already knew how I felt. I said, "How about we both make it or we both don't? That's the way it should be. Quick and dirty."

"You sure?"

"Why not?"

I looked at the bridge a long time, breathing deep, thinking about what I had to do. This time I wasn't going to tiptoe and get caught halfway, but I couldn't stomp across either—the bridge might be as fragile as the one before. I was going to try to go fast as I could, keeping it as smooth as I could. Better to go fast in case something happened.

I studied the bridge some more, stalling for time. I said to Raymond, "I've been thinking a lot about Johnny's letter, all the things he said."

"Me too."

"I forgot to ask you if you left it in the cabin where it could be found."

Raymond tapped his chest. "I've got it right in my pocket. I wanted to read it at the potlatch."

"Then we have to make it," I said. "Or what he said is all going to be lost."

"We'll make it. I have a feeling we're going to make it."

Then Raymond croaked like a raven, two, three times, a perfect imitation. The sound carried far in the cold air.

"Raven medicine," I said with a smile.

We waited then, savoring our friendship, knowing that everything could end in moments.

I asked Raymond if he was ready. He said, "Anytime, little brother."

I was ready too. Whatever happened, I thought, we'd done our best and you can't ask for more than that.

Go!

I started across, pulling hard as I could, trying to go fast without tripping myself up. I saw only the crust on the snow breaking into jigsaw pieces beneath my snowshoes. Right when I got to the far side of the bridge I heard it crack behind me. I never looked back; I broke into a run with the snowshoe tips high, heaving and exploding with everything I had, and then I felt myself going down. I lunged as far forward as I could, my face going down in a slab of snow.

Behind me I heard Raymond shouting for joy, and I looked up to see him in the toboggan right behind me. He was pointing downriver where the ice bridge was floating away.

I saw blood in the snow where I'd scratched up my face. I could have cared! I saw I'd broken one of my snowshoe frames. No matter! We still had Raymond's pair on the toboggan.

A half hour later the canyon walls began to dive down toward the river. Downstream, where they tailed into the river, we could see vapor rising from the right bank. "The hot springs," Raymond said.

There was no open water in the flat country beyond the canyons. Only distance to be closed, step by step, between us and that last isolated hogback of the Mackenzie Mountains that Nahanni Butte was named after. The village, Raymond said, sat barely above the river where

204

it touched the foot of that hogback on the right-hand side.

In the days to come, I kept my eyes fastened on that mountain. I had to believe it was getting closer because for a long, long time it didn't seem that way. I was all out of strength. I knew I'd lost track of time, and I lost touch with Raymond too, as the places I was going in my mind became much more real than the frozen, featureless landscape around me.

Toward the end, I thought I was wandering around the streets of Yellowknife. A lady asked me if I wanted to come in for some tea. I realized it was my mother. I said I would sure like that, and she had me sit down at the kitchen table and she served me rose hip tea and some chocolate chip cookies. There was a porcupine in the corner of the room that was chewing on the leg of a fancy china hutch. My mother said it didn't matter; it belonged to Johnny Raven. "This is Johnny Raven's house," she explained. "He'll be coming home in a few minutes from work." Then Johnny Raven came in, and he said he was glad to see me. I said, "Boy, am I glad to see you." I asked if he'd seen Raymond, and he said Raymond was back in the mountains; I could go find him there. Johnny said he would like me to stay and visit some more, but I said, "No thanks, I better get going if I'm going to catch up with Raymond." I hiked all the way back into the mountains, and I kept calling his name, but he couldn't hear me because the falls were too loud. Then at last I heard him calling *my* name. "Gabe!" he hollered. "Gabe, Gabe!"

My mind jerked back into consciousness. Raymond really was calling my name. I turned around and saw him there on the toboggan. "You fell asleep," he said, "standing up. You've been standing there for a long time."

It was twilight. "Look at that fog," I said blankly, and pointed toward a low bluff up ahead.

Raymond looked where I was pointing, looked again, and said, "That's smoke from everybody's stoves!"

"Stoves?" I mumbled.

He said, "That's the village, Gabe! We're almost there!"

It got dark on us that last stretch. I remember pulling by the light of a crescent moon.

At last Raymond steered me to the bottom of a thirty-foot slope on the right-hand side of the riverbed. "Stop," he said. "This is it."

"I don't see anything," I managed to say.

"It's right up above us, right here. We just can't see it."

It was only fog after all, I thought. Not the village.

"It's right up there," he said again. "Smell the woodsmoke."

I thought I could smell woodsmoke, but I knew I might be imagining it.

A dog appeared atop the slope, some sort of husky, and broke loose barking. I knew I didn't have enough left in me to climb that hill. Much too steep. Maybe after I rested . . .

"Maybe we should camp here," I said.

The dog kept barking. We heard someone yell at it to shut up. Raymond shouted, nobody heard. The dog kept barking. At last a human being appeared up there in the moonlight. A young boy. "Who is it?" he called, his voice thin and scared.

"It's Raymond."

"Who?"

"Jimmy, it's me! Raymond Providence!"

The boy turned and ran. Raymond said, "That's my little cousin Jimmy."

We waited, not very long. Within minutes, eighty-some people had run out, and they were all standing there on the top of the slope. They must've thought they were seeing ghosts. They weren't saying a word.

"It's me," Raymond said. "It's me, Raymond, and my friend Gabe."

A woman shrieked. Everybody came surging down the hill at once, and then they lifted us up and carried us into the village.

My father and I flew upstream over the frozen Liard River in a ski-equipped Cessna on the second of April. When we were still twenty miles from Nahanni Butte, I could recognize the shape of the hogback mountain. As we got closer we could see the village below with all its smoking chimneys. We could see cars and pickups crossing the Liard on the winter road, just upstream from where the Nahanni came in.

They came from Fort Simpson and Fort Liard and Fort Providence, from places like Red Knife River and Burnt Island and Slave Point. They came from all over, and they streamed into Nahanni Butte's community hall for Johnny Raven's potlatch.

It was warm inside, warm from the fire burning in the great fireplace and warm from being packed with nearly three hundred people. They sat at tables and on folding chairs and they stood all along the walls, all these Dene faces from infants to elders who could've been in their nineties.

These old ones, I realized, had lived most of their lives outdoors. Like Johnny's, their faces were worn like maps of rivers and mountains.

There was fiddle music and there was food, mountains of food, traditional and modern, set out on two rows of tables that stretched across one end of the great room. In the open kitchen behind the tables, we could see the hot food steaming.

Before anyone ate, there were stories to be told, stories of Johnny Raven. Most of the elders spoke in English, and they told of Johnny's life, the things he had done for people. They never failed to mention Johnny's great success as a hunter. They would pause as they spoke, and the elder who was the emcee, at a second mike, would translate what had been said into Slavey.

One bent old man with hair white as Johnny's got up and spoke in Slavey. The emcee was translating his story into English. The old man began by saying that what he was about to say was rarely spoken of, but unless he told it, people in the future would think that such things were only in the domain of legends. And then he told of accompanying Johnny Raven, when they both were young, on the last hunt of a grizzly with a spear. It was Johnny, he said, who spoke to the bear and called it Grandfather, called it out of its den, and planted the spear. It was because of Johnny's humility and worthiness, the old man said, that the great bear knew that its time had come and gave its life upon the spear.

When the old man was done he gave a piece of bear meat to the fire for Johnny's spirit, as other speakers had also given food to the flames.

There was a round of murmuring around the hall, in appreciation for what had been said and in anticipation of what was about to come. People seemed to know that Raymond was going to speak, and that he was going to speak last. The word had spread around the Dene country of Raymond's and my long ordeal in the mountains, and how it was the knowledge of an elder—Johnny Raven—that had made it possible for us to continue on our own.

We were in the folding chairs. Raymond was sitting on my left side, his foot and lower leg encased in a cast. He'd been home from the hospital in Edmonton for only a week. Next week he'd be joining me back in school at Yellowknife.

My father was on my right side. Raymond's family was all around us, his parents and his grandparents, his big sister, Monique, his little brother, Alfred, and his little sister, Dora—lots of other relatives too. I could feel their pride swelling, though they were trying not to show it. And I felt their fear for Raymond too, that he had decided he had to do this, stand up in front of so many people and speak. I heard his little sister, Dora, whisper what they were all feeling. "Raymond, aren't you afraid?"

Raymond's fingers were tapping nervously on Johnny's hand drum. He whispered to his sister, "I sure am!" Then he glanced to his parents, who whispered their encouragement. The elder who was introducing him had nearly finished. I picked Raymond's crutches up off the floor and got ready to hand them to him. Raymond whispered to me, "Gabe, how am I going to do this?"

He could hardly breathe. He looked pale. It was so warm in there in the first place, I thought he was going to faint.

I said, "Look at everything else you got through."

The speaker had finished talking now. All eyes in the

room were on Raymond, and a hush fell over the hall. He stood up, steadying himself on my shoulder as I handed him the crutches. He was set to go, and then he nodded toward the drum on the chair and said, "I want to have the drum with me. Come up there with me, Gabe."

We started across the open floor and steered toward the microphone. I was gimping alongside him, my knee still wrapped from my arthroscopic surgery in Yellow-knife. When we got all the way up there, I turned around and saw the same sea of faces that Raymond was look-ing at. I noticed the curiosity in the faces of the kids our age clustered together down at the end of the hall, still and expectant like everybody else.

The elder who had introduced Raymond set up a fold-ing chair for me to sit on. Raymond had freed up his right hand as he leaned forward on the crutches. His glance told me he wanted the drum. He held it in his right hand by the woven spruce roots that ran across its back. I heard him take a deep breath as I turned to sit down.

"This is Johnny's drum," Raymond began.

He didn't say it very loud, and his voice was shaky. But everybody heard him.

"I'm sure Johnny made a lot of drums in his life," Raymond said a little louder. "This was his last drum. A wolverine got after it and tore the skin."

Everybody laughed.

Raymond was surprised. He didn't know they were going to laugh. He relaxed. "So I made a new one for it."

I thought he would open Johnny's letter right away. It was in the envelope that was sticking out of his shirt pocket. Instead he began to talk about Johnny, how he never really knew his great-uncle. Then he said that he was lucky to get to know him in the last two months of his life. He said he was going to tell about Johnny's last two months so everybody would know what he did.

Everyone in the hall listened intently as Raymond told his story, pausing to let the elder translate into Slavey. When he told of the airplane going over the falls, there was a gasp. He told what happened as we ran out of patience waiting for a search plane, how the two of us decided to build the raft and escape. He told of Johnny thinking it wasn't such a good idea, and his sorrow over leaving most of the moose meat behind. The old people around the hall were nodding their heads, understanding perfectly.

In every face in that room, I could see them imagining it all happening way back there in the mountains. I could feel Raymond's confidence growing.

Raymond told how we were stranded in Deadmen Valley. He told how Johnny kept hunting even when he knew all the moose had probably left. He told of Johnny building the snowshoes. I could see Raymond's parents hanging on every word, my father too. My dad was sitting up to his full height, solemn and respectful as if he was at church, sneaking glances at me as if still trying to convince himself that I was indeed alive. I smiled thinking how it turned out I was right when I guessed he was in that airplane we'd heard flying above the clouds when we were down in the canyon on the raft.

Raymond told of Johnny leading us to the frozen beaver pond after our hope was all but gone. The people were hushed, listening intently. When Raymond told of pulling the beavers out onto the ice, a cry of joy and triumph went up from an old woman down by the kitchen, and applause began from the kids down on the other end of the hall. The applause grew and grew until it sounded like thunder.

When at last the applause had died down, Raymond said, "Johnny died soon after that."

Raymond took the envelope from his shirt pocket, took out Johnny's letter, gave a brief explanation of how we came by it, and began to read.

Raymond read it simply, humbly. I thought how it wasn't Raymond reading; to me it sounded just like Johnny talking, Johnny telling of his love for the land and his hopes for the young people. At the end, when Johnny said, "I miss the taste of moose tongue and beaver tail," there were smiles and laughter all around the hall. Then Raymond finished with Johnny's last words: "And so I say to you: take care of the land, take care of yourself, take care of each other."

The hall was profoundly quiet in the wake of Johnny's last words. Raymond turned and made his way on the crutches to the fireplace, clutching the hand drum with a couple of fingers. One of the elders brought up a TV tray with big straps of bear fat heaped on it. Raymond beckoned me over with a wave of his head. I took the drum so he could free his right hand. With a little toss, he threw a big strap of fat into the fire, and it started sizzling. He looked at it intently, and then he turned to me and said, "You too, Gabe."

I placed another strap of fat in the fire. Raymond's head was bowed. I was remembering Johnny's gentle face in the firelight as he told the old stories, sang the old songs. I could see him peeling back the flakes of pine bark and showing us where the camprobbers hid their blueberries. He was looking at the two of us, and he was smiling. "Thank you, Johnny," I whispered. The silence in the room held another few minutes, and then everybody was streaming toward the tables filled with food.